Fists and boots slammed into him all at once, knocking the wind out of him, bloodying his face.

John kicked the man with the sunglasses in his knee, breaking it instantly. The man fell backwards, bumping into a few fighting thugs, knocking them back to the floor with him.

John saw his chance. He caught the combat boot of one creep and pushed him backwards, sending him flying through the air. He rolled away from stomping boots and jumped up quickly. The thugs didn't miss a beat. Within seconds they circled him, but he was ready for them this time.

Knuckles from everywhere smashed into his head, face, and body. John put his hands up and swung on them, knocking a few out, beating one to the floor. Then he beat two. Then three. He was fighting the entire Pool Hall now, throwing haymakers at the mob, catching a few himself.

Vince the bar tender leaped over the bar and rushed towards him with a bat. He took a mighty swing—

—and missed John as he ducked. He hit two thugs instead, knocking them into a table where three civilians were sitting. Frightened patrons who had nothing to do with the fracas took off like bats out of hell, running out of the place.

OUTLAW

CITY OF FEAR

JOSHUA SARGENT

For my true friends: Andy Hyter, Marcus Goodman, Krisjohn Jones, and Christine Wong.

To Pete

Do not walk in the way with them, keep your foot from their path; for their feet run to evil, and they make haste to shed blood.

—Proverbs 1:16

PROLOGUE

BLOOD MONEY

Michael Priest took the cocaine out of his pocket and piled it on the mirror. He cut himself two huge lines, then rolled up a dollar bill and took a hit. The drip. He loved the drip. He absolutely *loved* it; when the coke numbed the back of this throat. His heart felt like it was going to jump out of his chest. His head was about to explode. So be it.

Rats the size of phone books scurried past his black boots. Oblivious to the piss and vomit smell around him he leaned back in the shitty blue couch, enjoying his high. He sat in the crack house, unafraid. Unafraid of the world. BayView was his, no one dared touch him here. He owned this city.

Gunshots rang out as the gang war continued outside. Screaming and automatic gunfire echoed throughout KingStreet. Unmindful of dying voices and bullets flying through the windows he kept his eyes closed.

The room spun out of control as he leaned forward and sniffed up more coke on the cracked piece of mirror. The white was all over his black leather pants, the excess powder falling off of his chin, sprinkling his boots. He closed his eyes and rested his head on the couch, his spiked mohawk mashing against the cushion.

Sailing. Sailing far, far away. The only thing that could blow his high was that annoying fuck face Bobby Keys. Sniveling cocksucker was whimpering as he sat tied to the chair across the room. What Bobby failed to understand was that he was in charge. The streets were his, nobody made a move or sold even a dime bag without his say so. He'd make him understand. He owned this city.

To make things worse, Priest was getting angry. Trash, Psycho, and Danny Boy were behind him, arguing. They were all out of ideas on how to make Bobby pay up. He blinked his eyes open and jumped up from the couch, startling even his own underlings.

He leaped over it and ordered Danny Boy to make Bobby tell him where the money was. The broad-shouldered man nodded. He ran across the room and untied Keys, snatched him up, and started beating the hell out of him.

He glared at Trash and Psycho, feeling the sudden urge to pummel them both to death. Tense seconds passed, Bobby's thrashing being the only sound in the room. The urge to kill them passed. He moved to the front of the couch, slumped down, and snorted some more.

He leaned back and shook violently, his blue eyes rolling back into his head. The sounds of screaming and ribs being cracked echoed in his head as Danny Boy went to work.

Nobody could touch his crew. Anyone who had dared had been crushed to a pulp. Though his head danced with powder his mind was still on murder. All the powder in the world didn't change the fact that he had enemies. They were out there. Watching. Waiting. Waiting for the opportunity to take over.

He wouldn't let that happen. He would cut the head of every man who tried to make a move. Blood would flow in the streets by his word until they all bowed to him. He stopped shaking and snatched up the bag of dope. He poured out some more and took another hit.

He wiped his nose and got up, taking his time moving across the room. Danny was bashing the weeping man to a pulp. He pushed the intimidating thug aside and took a twelve-inch hunting knife out of his jacket pocket.

Priest barked at Psycho, demanding his lighter. He stood Bobby up and grinned, enjoying the sight of his bloody, broken nose and busted lips. Bobby was *going* to tell him where the money was, even if it took all day. He gave his knife to Psycho and told him to heat the blade up, grinning the whole time.

Satisfied that it was hot enough he snatched it and grabbed Keys by the neck. Trash and Danny Boy held his arms. Priest slowly moved the knife closer to Bobby's face, cackling wildly as he did it.

Terror swept over him when it was near his eye. Two inches away. One inch away. He yelled out in agony as the hot blade pierced his iris, slowly moving deeper into his eye. Priest could care less. Should've paid up. He roared louder when Bobby's right eye exploded, blood and milky fluid leaking from his empty socket.

Bobby Keys wailed like a burning dog as the thugs let him go. Michael gave a damn about his wailings, he stared at him indifferently as he crashed to the floor, screaming like a little girl. He staggered back to the filthy couch, back to the beloved white that awaited him.

There had to be some way to make Keys talk. There just *had* to. That money belonged to him, that's what he and everyone else in this filth hole failed to understand. He put the bill to his nose and tried to think…then stopped himself when he remembered his Louisville Slugger under the couch. He smiled wickedly, letting the dollar bill drop to the table.

Michael Priest *owned* this city. BayView was his.

ONE

BLOOD POURED OUT OF JOHN'S FACE AND mouth as he balled his fists up and swung on his attackers. The gang surrounded him outside of Martin Luther King highschool, and there was no way out. They had him in a vicious circle, hitting him with bats, slashing him with knives and razors. One of the thugs took a swing at him, but he dodged it. He swung and landed a vicious right on his chin, knocking him out cold. Another pulled out a switchblade and took a step toward him.

"I'm gonna kill you!"

He recognized the voice immediately. It was Pug, leader of the South Side Boys. Pug and his crew had had it in for him for weeks, and now it looked like they were going to get their chance to off him.

Pug took a swipe at John's neck, missing it by inches. He drew the blade back, cutting the left side of his face instead. He grabbed him by the wrist and broke his arm with a sickening snap that echoed in his ears. Pug cried out in agony and curled up on the floor.

It was a fight for survival now. John picked up a brick and hurled it into the murderous group, smashing it into one hood's face. Three of them were down now and he fought the other three, kicking them, punching them, slamming one of them into the brick building. The fourth one he didn't see.

The last thug slowly walked up from behind, pulling out a .38 pistol. John turned around out of instinct, but it was too late. The gun was already in his face.

"Sweet dreams," the boy said, and squeezed the trigger.

John felt a hand nudging his shoulder. A soft voice called out to him.

"Sir? Sir are you alright?"

He blinked his eyes open and glanced around frantically. He wasn't even at MLK High. He was sitting on an airplane, and an attractive woman with soft brown skin and black, flowing hair was softly shaking him awake. He eased a little when he saw her.

A dream. It was only a dream.

John Cutter closed his eyes again and wiped his forehead with the back of his hand. He ignored the stinging sweat that leaked into his green eyes. His brown skin was beaded with perspiration, his face and upper lip dotted with it. The white t-shirt he was wearing stuck to his body. He squeezed the dog tags that were around his neck, and said a silent prayer of thanks before opening his eyes. He'd made it.

No matter how long ago the fight went down, John still remembered being jumped like it was yesterday.

Denver Colorado was a nice place, but MLK was a dangerous school. That was one of the reasons his parents urged him to go to College. Since he'd been a bright kid he'd been bullied for most of his childhood. Kids had teased him, claiming he didn't sound 'Black enough when he talked,' so he'd fought regularly for it. By the time he'd become a teenager rival gangs began terrorizing all the high schools, using extortion and dope to come up. Not wanting him to fall in with the wrong crowd Mr. Cutter wanted to protect his son, so he got him into positive activities. At the young age of eleven he'd enrolled his son into Kay's Boxing Gym, a place where he had spent most of his young life after school. Things were looking up for John. Kids had stopped teasing him because of his boxing and he'd even became popular after awhile. He had also befriended a couple of tough youths. Despite the fact that he'd graduated MLK at sixteen his parents had stayed on his ass about everything; they didn't like his clothes or his new *friends*, his girlfriend in particular. After a few arguments with his folks he'd ran away from home. He lied about his age and joined the Army, did a few tours and fought against the Falcon Rebels in the jungles of Brazil, where he was wounded in combat. The Army gave him an Honorable Discharge, and he'd visited his parents for a few weeks in Colorado.

Yeah I made it, but it seems like my nightmares have gotten worse, he thought.

The combined memories of being slashed in the face and almost getting his ass blown off in the war was enough to last him a lifetime. Doctors from Walter Reed didn't seem to help much. And the medication was a joke. He was diagnosed with Post Traumatic Stress, and ordered to see over a dozen shrinks and specialists. The two gunshots in his chest from a firefight could have been fatal, but luckily he'd escaped with his life after saving a few of his combat buddies. When Walter Reed was done with him he'd received the last of his orders, and his time in the U.S. Army was over.

To make things worse he'd gotten radiation poisoning in Brazil. He'd felt sick, but that wore off in a few days. For some strange reason he'd felt stronger, but the fact that he had been poisoned still bothered him, and doctor's found small traces in his body. He reached inside of his pocket and pulled out a piece of gum. A wallet-sized picture fell to the ground, and he paused for second. He picked it up, staring at it for a moment.

Charlie...

It was a picture of him and another soldier. They were standing in front of a tank, holding their M-16s. Rage boiled inside him as the photograph trembled in his hand. He could feel the heat rise to his face when he thought about how Charlie had made it out, too. His friend had received his orders to go home before he did. Though he'd survived combat, he was mysteriously gunned down in BayView City, a place that John had never heard of. He didn't know why he was killed in the strange place, but he was sure as hell going to find out. He got word of Charlie's death through the grapevine and took the first flight out of KDEN.

From what he saw on the Channel 6 News the Bayview Police Department were looking into his murder. So far they hadn't come up with anything, but assured the public that they were going to find the individuals responsible for the fatal shooting. Chief Duncan told reporters that he had some of his best men on the case, and urged Charlie's family and friends to be patient and let them do their jobs.

Fuck that. I'm going to do my own investigation and see what's what. they're gonna pay for what they did.

"Don't worry Charlie," he whispered under his breath as he squeezed the picture in his hand. "I'll find them."

The woman who'd woke him up earlier was staring at him like he was some kind of Martian from outer space. John straightened in his seat and stuffed the picture into his pocket. He leaned back and closed his eyes. He tried to sleep, but images of the Falcon War flashed in his mind.

"Sir, we're going to be serving lunch in about thirty minutes," a female stewardess dressed in dark blue said to him. "Would you like to have the chicken with rice?"

He stared at her blankly for a moment, then turned away. He slowly shook his head, his mind still off in a far away place. Closing his eyes, he tried to go back to sleep. He thought about what his mother had said to him when he went back home.

"Welcome home, baby. I, I thought about you every day. I prayed and prayed that you would come back. You haven't changed a bit. You're still my handsome son, even with that scar on your...well let's not talk about that. You're home now. We are so proud of you."

He felt guilty when he told her he had to go away again. He'd hated leaving like that, she'd only seen him for a week, but when Charlie was murdered he had to find some answers. Going to BayView was the only thing on his mind. He wouldn't be able to rest until he avenged his friend. He said his goodbyes to his parents, then left.

John knew that there was no way he'd be able to get back to sleep. He shifted in his seat and waited for the long flight to end.

TWO

JOHN WIPED HIS FACE AS HE stepped out of the airport and into the dark, summer night. The humid air hit him like waves of heat in a steam room. Sweat rolled down his torso and back as he stepped off the curb. He hailed down a cab.

"Where ya headed, buddy?" The cabby that pulled up was a middle-aged man with a ruddy, round face and a plaid cap on. He was dressed in a long-sleeved white shirt, and an antique gold watch was around his wrist.

"KingStreet." John picked up his duffel bag and headed to the back of the yellow taxi. The cabby popped the trunk and got out to help him.

"How long ya in town for?" The cab driver took his green duffel and loaded it into the trunk. He noted the puzzled look on his face when he said he was headed into KingStreet.

"Not long," John answered, not in the mood for conversation. The driver slammed the trunk down hard a few times, cursing the car's locking mechanism. After the fifth slam he ran to the front and hopped in.

John jumped into the back seat and pulled his door shut. He stared out of the window in silence as the Cabby sped off.

"The name's Nick," he said, eyeing him in his rearview. "What's your's, buddy?"

"John." He glanced away from the window.

Nick quickly looked away from his mirror when John stared at him. He turned his head and gazed out at the flash of people and city life as the taxi sped down the street, catching each light before it turned red. Bright orange and yellow lights flashed before his eyes as the car whipped by.

"So," Nick started, obviously trying to engage him in mindless chatter, "what brings you to BayView? You on personal business?"

"Yeah."

"Well, it's a great city, despite what ya hear. They call it the 'Bay' because the bridge is near the water."

"Is that a fact," he said, noting the familiar accent in his voice.

Nick sped up to beat the red light. He drove over the bridge and nodded towards the city's bay. "Me I'm from Brooklyn, born and raised. Lived there for thirty years, my friend. Then I moved out here! I needed a change of scenery, ya understand? I know it's the city out here, too, but some things kind of happened and I thought it was best I left town for awhile, ya know what I'm saying?"

"Yeah," John said, smirking, "I know how that is."

"Say John, you wouldn't happen to be from the mid-west, would ya?"

"Yup."

"I knew it!" He chuckled and slapped his knee. "I could hear it in your voice, my friend! A couple of yous guys came through the city a few times, and I could spot ya a mile away. Knew a guy named Ricky, he was from the mid-west. Don't know if you know Ricky."

"Nah man, I never heard of him."

"Well anyways, Ricky was a good guy. Kind of an asshole, but he was okay, that was just his way I suppose. He was from…say, where you from again?"

"I lived in Montbello."

"Oh." Nick's forehead creased for a second, and suddenly the inside of the cab grew very silent.

John stared at him from the backseat and smiled at that. He'd gotten that response a lot when he told people where he was from. People were often shocked when he'd told them where he was from because of Montbello's tough reputation. It had made the news over dozens of times, especially in the early eighties. He'd grown used to it when he'd joined the Army and told the other soldiers about his good ol' home. He'd even looked forward to telling them when they'd asked, just to see that stupid look on their faces. His smile faded when he thought about Brooks.

Sergeant Brooks was a hard-nosed drill instructor who'd trained him during boot camp. He was a bald-headed asshole with no life. For ten weeks he'd made life a living hell for John, always ragging on him about something. The delightful Sergeant was one of those rage-a-holics who was bitter about life, and hated his own kind. He knew the real reason why; Brooks hated him because he grew up middle-class. He was young and obviously going somewhere in his life. On one occasion, he'd remembered one of Brooks's many colorful conversations with him during training.
"Private Cutter! Get yo' ass in here!"
"Yes Drill Sergeant! This is Private Cutter, reporting his…"
"Shut up! You come from a rich family, don't ya?"
"Rich in spirit."
"Now you know what I mean, you know *doggone well* what I mean! You're friends had money, didn't they?"
"No Drill Sergeant!"
"You're best friend was rich, wasn't he?"
"No Drill Sergeant."
"You got a rich girlfriend, don't ya?"
"I don't have a girlfriend anymore, sir—"
"Yeah but I bet if ya' had a choice now she would be rich, wouldn't she?"
"…Permission to leave, Drill Sergeant."
"Make like Micah Jackson…and beat it."

Asshole John thought as he fidgeted with his seatbelt. He couldn't count how many times he'd wanted to hit Brooks in his cock-sucking mouth. What he couldn't understand was why he'd singled him out like that; just because he didn't grow up like Brooks did didn't give him the right to treat him like garbage. It had seemed like the Sergeant had always found a reason to mess with him.

It always bothered him how people put so much emphasis on things like that. John liked everyone, no matter what their race, class, or culture was. He thought it was stupid to judge someone because of their background.

"Okay pal, we're here!" Nick announced, slowing the car in front of a run-down motel.

John hopped out the cab. He noticed that Nick wasn't too quick to get out at first, and that his knuckles had turned white as he gripped the steering wheel for dear life. He popped the trunk so the young soldier could get his heavy duffel bag out. In front of the Sun Tree Motel stood a group of ruff-looking characters huddled around the entrance. They had spiked mohawks and the letter *A* was spray-painted on their t-shirts and leather jackets. They reminded him of those rock stars from the eighties he'd seen on those music documentaries.

The five punks turned around and mad-dogged him, their stares unwelcoming. Ignoring them he shouldered his awkward duffel, reached inside of his pocket, and made his way to Nick's window.

"Hey listen mac," Nick said, his voice tight and uneasy, "I gotta be gettin' back on the highway, ya' know? My wife's at home, and, and I live all the way uptown, so—"

He shook his head and cut him off. "No sweat," he said, handing him a hundred dollar bill, "I can carry my own bag."

"Listen John, I don't know if I have—"

He waved his hand. "Keep the change. Don't worry about it."

"Thanks, mac." The cabby smiled, exposing yellow-coffee-stained teeth.

Before he could even blink Nick took off like a shot, his tires screeching madly into the night. John turned around, continuing to ignore the fools who were grilling him with their beady eyes.

The sidewalk and street was covered with trash, the broken glass and hypodermic needles crunching under his feet as he made his way up the concrete stairs of the motel. Bullet holes and graffiti decorated the walls and glass doors to the main entrance. A majority of the tags looked like the same symbols the young hooligans wore on their clothes. Behind him he could hear them muttering curses under their breath, no doubt directed towards him. In the distance he also heard the feint sounds of gun fire and punk rock music.

Inside of the raggedy motel, a small man with narrow eyes stood behind the check-in counter. Sweat rolled down his round face, and he combed his mustache with his index finger. He was reading the BayView Times.

"I need a room for tonight."

The man glanced up from his paper, eyeing John suspiciously. He could see that the man's hair was thinning in the front and middle of his head, the light shining off of his bald scalp. The nametag on his black vest read Mr. Lang, and there was a quarter-sized mustard stain on the middle of his white, collared shirt.

"Rooms are seventy-eight for night," he said, clearing his throat before he went on, "and cable TV is out."

He sighed heavily and stared at Mr. Lang. He wasn't in the mood for any mess tonight because he didn't feel like walking to another motel. *Come on you old bastard, just take the money and gimme a room.* To his relief he took it, then turned around and moved from behind the counter.

"The money is due when I say it is, and I don't want it late. If you have to go in or out it doesn't matter. I don't care. But I tell you this time. No trouble. I see trouble, I'll throw you out. You understand?"

"Yeah man, I got it."

John followed him upstairs. Along the way were a few dead roaches curled up on the ground. Dwarf rats the size of small dogs were gnawing away at a rotten slice of pizza. He made it to his room, eyed it up and down, and took in what he saw when the lights came on. Not the best looking bed as far a beds go, but he was hungry, tired, and frustrated. All he could think about was finding someone who knew Charlie, and how he was going to get to the bottom of this.

"No noise at night. I don't want to hear anything after eight o'clock. Understand?"

"Yeah," John answered, sighing deeply, "I understand."

And with that, Lang turned and vanished downstairs. John sat down on his raggedy bed, the white covers stained with green and brown spots. On top of his night stand was a worn out copy of the Holy Bible, the black leather cover withered and peeled back. A red roach the size of an I-pod skittered past his feet, crawled up the wall on the other side of the room, then disappeared into one of the cracks.

Little roach bastard.

John yanked the dirty blanket and white covers off of the bed. He balled them up and threw them into the beaten-up wooden chair behind him. There was no way in hell he was going to sleep with those filthy covers on the goddamn bed, they were probably crawling with disease and God knows what else. He reached up to turn the lights out and drifted off into an uneasy sleep.

THREE

KA—BOOM!
A loud explosion from outside jolted John awake, and for a split second he thought he was back in Brazil, fighting the Falcon Army. He sprang from his bed, the edgy panic seeping down into his soul. Sweat oozed from every pore of his body.
Boom! Boom!
At the sound of shotgun blasts, he hit the floor and crawled over to his duffel that was next to the bathroom doorway. His heart thundered in his chest as he expected a bullet to crash through his window. Ignoring the roaches that skittered towards him, he reached out for his green bag, and yanked it towards him.

He reached inside it and snatched out his black pair of Levis' jeans, a fresh white t-shirt, and his black Air Force 1's. With lightening speed he dressed, crouching the whole time as two bullets shattered his window.
Where the fuck am I, Beirut?
He tied his shoes up with shaky fingers and tried to control his breathing. Tucking his dog tags inside of his shirt he crept out of his room, closed the door behind him, and moved down the hallway with the cunningness of a ninja. Much to his surprise every door to his right and left was shut tight. He knew that he was in a shitty part of town, and wondered if the poor people who stayed here were used to this sort of thing.
Rat-tat-tat! Rat-tat-tat!
Bullets whizzed over his head, missing him by mere inches, peppering the wall to his left. More followed, and he

ran down the stairs, shielding the side of his face with his forearm as he went. The main lobby was a mess. The dark-brown table and wooden chair he'd seen propped up against the wall before was now in a million pieces. He glanced over at the front desk, noticing that Mr. Lang was nowhere in sight. He took a deep breath, exhaled sharply, then forced himself through the main entrance.

Chaos surrounded him when he stepped outside. Fifty feet ahead of him to the right was the Taco Times Restaurant he'd seen last night. It'd looked in perfect shape, and was the only semi-decent looking hang-out on KingStreet. Now it was engulfed in fire. Soaring flames danced over twenty feet high, bellowing out of the broken windows of the ruined establishment.

John watched in awe as a man burst through the burning door of the restaurant. He was on fire, screaming in agony as the flames swirled around him, scorching the flesh from his bones. A burbling cry rose from the man's throat as he continued to roast alive, flailing his arms wildly, spinning in the street in circles. He fell on his knees and collapsed. Loud popping sounds like meat being cooked on a grill came from the man's body, and he didn't rise again.

Twenty feet ahead of the Hao Long restaurant stood nine punks with green-spiked mohawks. Some had metal pipes. Others carried switchblades, and John could see the panic on their faces as a dozen hoods on motorcycles circled them like vultures. The bikers were screaming at them, taunting them with insults and throwing up their middle fingers. One of the punks gripped his metal pipe and stepped forward.

"Fuck RGC! Punks forever!"

The Punk charged forward and took a swing at one of the circling bikers, knocking him off of his Harley Davidson. The biker fell to the ground with a mighty thud and the powerful machine skidded sideways, crashing into a blue

Cutlass parked on the side of the street. The other Punks followed suit, but they were no match for the bikers.

    Out of nowhere, ten more riders materialized. They hopped off of their mighty machines and rushed the outnumbered Punks, kicking and stomping them to the unforgiving street. Chains and crescent wrenches were pulled. They pummeled the spike-haired goons with countless blows. A lone biker in sunglasses screeched from around the corner, a Molotov cocktail in his hand. He sped towards the Taco Times and hurled the burning glass at the building, fueling the already raging fire.

    John jumped up on the curb to avoid being run over by the crazed motorcyclist. A sinking feeling crept inside of him. His internal alarms went off like crazy, and every hair on the back of his neck stood when he glanced down at the asphalt, and noticed two sets of shadows; his, and someone else's. Somebody was behind him.

    By the time John turned around, it was too late. Something heavy struck the side of his head, knocking him to the floor. Sharp pain throbbed in his skull and the left side of his cheek. He could feel hot liquid running down the top left side of his head. Blood. Definitely blood. And he had a feeling that he was going to lose a lot of it.

    John glanced up at his attacker. A man well over six feet towered over him. His mohawk was different from the other Punks. The yellow spikes were higher, the color of the tips orange. His black, diamond-studded-leather-jacket matched his pants, and his large combat boots looked like they could crush a man's skull with one stomp. Tucked in his diamond-studded belt was a 9-mm pistol, and his muscle definition was visible through his white t-shirt. A malicious smile spread across the man's rugged face, and before he could react, the large Punk swung his mighty bat again, striking him across his face and hitting his eye.

    John cringed from the impact of the blow. A queasy

feeling knotted his stomach, and he prepared himself for the worst possible pain. To his surprise, he didn't feel any.

No way, that second blow shoulda' killed me! What's going on?

He wasn't about to give him a second chance to swing on him. The towering Punk rose the bat over his head, but John rolled to his right, avoiding the attack. A metallic *ting* sounded as the thug struck the asphalt, missing his head.

"Kill that motherfucker, Priest!" A man's voice boomed from the chaos around him.

More shouts of his execution rose from different Punks as they piled out of alleyways and various buildings, carrying bats and broken pipes with them. John turned and hit Priest in the stomach with his fist, then delivered a quick uppercut to his chin followed by a left hook to his jaw. Stunned, Priest staggered back, still clutching the bat in his hands. His wide, blue eyes looked glassy, like he was about to drop any minute, and John saw his chance. He rushed the dazed thug, pummeling him with body blows and combinations.

Priest swung at him wildly, but he was too slow. John ducked each aimless swing and came up with a finishing uppercut, sending him to the ground. He stepped back and kept his hands up, eyeing him for any movement. The Punk wasn't getting up any time soon.

Behind John an angry mob of Anarchy members hurried towards him, their faces twisted into mortal scowls. He ran to Priest's side and scooped up his bat, then turned and knocked them away as they surrounded him. The twelve Punks had him in a circle, and he knew he was going to have to fight his way out. One by one he smashed them with their own leader's weapon until all twelve lay crumpled on the ground, doubling over in pain. With one free hand he wiped at the left side of his face, and looked down at his bloody palm.

Damn, I need a hospital. This is too much blood…

His stomach turned at the sight of the pooling blood in

his hand, dripping down his fingers, dotting the street beneath him in puddles of red. He wondered how deep the wound was and yearned for a mirror. He blinked his eyes once and snapped out of it. Now was not the time to worry about it, he could get to a mirror later.

All around him, a full-scale gang war had erupted between RGC and the Anarchy crew. The Punks were fighting hard, but taking the major end of the beating. A huge biker hurled one of them through a shop window, then turned around and smashed another one in the face with his massive fist, knocking him backwards to the gritty sidewalk. Everywhere he looked Punks were getting kicked, stomped, and beaten to the pavement. All except one.

Priest had recovered from John's beating. He was on his feet, slugging it out with three beefy RGC cronies. The young veteran watched in shock as he knocked out two of them with a mighty hammer fist. He picked up a brick and clocked the third biker square in the nose. Bright-red blood gushed everywhere as he staggered from the blow and fell to the ground. He hurled the brick at a passing cyclist, cursing loudly the whole time.

Three Punks cornered a young-looking woman at the Village Thrift Store behind John. They were cussing at her, waving broken bottles in her face. One of them cocked his hand back and knocked her to the floor. The other two inched forward, preparing to stomp her into the ground.

John took off towards the woman's direction, hoping to reach her in time. He reached them with amazing speed. Leaping in the air he dove into them, knocking them into the brick wall of the thrift store. He cocked his fist back and punched the ugly face of one, breaking his jaw instantly. The other two leaped to their feet and took off running, disappearing down the alleyway between the Pawn Shop and the thrift store.

A young thug ran out of the thrift store and stood in

front of John, a Louisville Slugger clutched in his hands. One fatal swing, and his brains would be all over the street. The Punk had a green-spiked mohawk, and 'Anarchy' was painted on his long-sleeve, ripped-white shirt. He was decked out in combat boots and black jeans. A winged dragon was tattooed on his neck. With all his might he kicked the Punk in his chest, sending him flying backwards. The back of his head hit the concrete, knocking him out instantly.

John ran over to the unconscious Punk. He grabbed his wooden baseball bat and swung on the oncoming crowd of Punks, knocking a few of them to the floor.

FWOOOSH!

The taco restaurant exploded, bricks and debris littering the ground. A large orange fireball spewed outwards, churning towards the sky as thick black clouds of smoke billowed upwards. Eleven Punks in blue jeans, leather jackets, and boots emerged from around the corner with weapons in their hands.

John reached out and helped the young woman to her feet. She looked to be in her early twenties. Her smooth, tanned skin indicated that she was from out west somewhere, probably California. Behind him he could feel one of the bastard Punks running up on him. He pushed the woman out of the way, then ducked out of instinct. He looked up to see a metal pipe go over his head. He threw a crushing elbow to the Punk's chest, then knocked him up side the head with the bat. Another swing split the thug's face open from his forehead to his bottom lip, and that was all it took. The hooligan fell to the floor with a mighty thud.

John turned around and sprinted over to the woman he had rescued seconds ago. Her huge, hazel-gray eyes reflected shock. Sweat had blanketed her face and drenched her long, straight, jet-black hair that stopped at her shoulders. He handed her the Slugger.

"Come on," he said, "we can't stay here. It's too dangerous in the streets, we gotta find cover."

The young woman motioned with her free hand down the street. "This way! We can make it to Montebello Street if we use the subway! I have a place, we can hide out there."

John and the woman made their way down the mayhem of KingStreet, steering clear of the various gang brawls. To the left of them was the Good Times Cineplex. It looked like it had been burned down for months, the blackened rubble and bricks littering the floor of the gutted theatre. Ahead of it was the High Times Liquor store.

"That's Mr. Luigi's store," the woman said. "Looks like he's not in today because of the—"

Rat-tat-tat!

Whatever she was about to say was cut short by the automatic gunfire that came from the upper window of High Times. A crazed, shirtless man with a green mohawk was hanging out of the window, firing his M-16 into the fighting crowd of bikers. Punks and riders alike scattered, searching for cover. John and the young woman ducked and sprinted towards the subway entrance as the lone gunman continued his rampage. Bullets ricochet off of the sidewalks and shattered parked cars all along the violent streets.

BOOM! Click, click...

They stopped dead in their tracks and spun around. They looked up to see that the lone gunman had dropped his gun. He let out a blood-curdling yell and fell from the window, dropping to the ground. A large biker with dark sunglasses and a full beard stood off to the side, holding a smoking sawed-off in his brawny hands. Priest was standing forty feet away from the biker.

"Houston!"

Cal Houston whipped around and faced Priest, his shotgun aimed dead at his face. Both men had their guns raised, ready to blow each other to hell.

"It's time to pay Michael," Houston said, a smile spreading across his grizzly face. "You can't run forever."

Michael Priest took a step forward and tightened his finger around the trigger. "You want the money? Fine. You can take it from my cold, dead fingers."

It was a stand-off. They sighted each other with their guns. Neither one was about to back down. Neither one looked like they were considering losing face in front of their followers. No, there was only one way that this was going to end; neither one of them walking away.

"Who the fuck you think you fuckin' with, Houston? You think you can fuckin' shake me down? KingStreet is *mine!*"

Angry police sirens blared in the distance, and sounded like they were getting closer. They both paused for a moment, their fingers on their triggers. Priest's eyes burned with contempt, his face scarlet.

"We'll meet again, Michael." Houston smiled wide, exposing yellow, rotten teeth. "And next time, there will be no interruptions."

As soon as John blinked Cal Houston had vanished. Priest tucked his pistol and ran towards the Village Thrift Store, then disappeared down the alley. The sirens were getting louder, and the bikers scrambled towards their Harleys for a fast get-away.

"That's our cue," John said, nodding at the woman he'd saved.

Two large poles six feet wide and thirty feet high stood to the right of them, ten feet apart from each other. A subway train rumbled forward, shaking the ground. The train doors hissed open, and they boarded it in haste.

FOUR

JOHN SAT NEXT TO THE WOMAN IN silence as the train rumbled along the tracks. Flashes of lights zipped by as they sped through the tunnels, waiting to get to the other side. She turned to him.

"I'm April Azzone," she said, letting out a shaky sigh. "Thanks for saving my life back there."

He nodded but said nothing, staring out of the window at the flashing lights. A poster of the newest rapper hung from a tunnel wall. The train's walls were decorated with rival gang graffiti, and the floors beneath them reeked of piss. Hypodermic needles and half-smoked spliffs littered the floor. He frowned at an old newspaper, then stared at her a moment.

April was a very attractive woman. From sizing her up he guessed she was about five-feet-ten, around a buck fifty. She had on a dark-blue, tight fitted t-shirt that matched her pants. Her cargo pants were snug around her thighs, and she had on black tennis shoes. She was athletic, he could tell she kept in good shape. He reached inside of his pocket and pulled out the picture.

"I have to ask you something." He handed it to her. "A few days ago a good friend of mine was killed right here in BayView. On KingStreet, as a matter of fact. Now I came here to find out who did it. Can you help me?"

She took the photograph from him, rubbing her soft chin as she glanced at it. Her eyes widened.

"I've seen this man before!" Her voice rose in pitch. "As a matter of fact I met him outside of Mr. Lang's motel. I was there the night he was killed."

He felt a rush of adrenaline, and for a second, he

thought this just might be the break he was looking for. "Can you tell me what you saw?"

She gave it back to him. "Some guys were arguing outside of the motel. As I said I was there to visit Lang when all the craziness started. In fact, two men were arguing with Priest."

"Priest?"

She nodded slowly. "Michael Priest. The man you were fighting with earlier. He's the leader of the Anarchy Gang, also known as the Punks. They control all of KingStreet, and they're at war with every crew."

He eyed her curiously. "I don't understand."

She pointed to the graffiti on the walls. "BayView's most violent gangs have been fighting over the drug trade for years now. Three months ago Priest was at war with the Gutter Street Mafia. He won the fight and started shaking down their turf on Riverside. He also went against other crews, putting word out on the streets that they can either pay him a cut, or die. Rather than fight with Anarchy, everybody decided to play ball and pay them off. Everybody except for those bikers. I don't know who they are, though."

John leaned forward and covered his mouth with his fist. *How did Charlie get mixed up in all of this* he thought. Charlie never hurt another living soul. He was the type of person who always kept his nose clean and stayed to himself.

"Anyway," April continued, "two strangers came to Priest's turf, and started arguing with him over money. I heard someone say "It's time, Michael," and Priest went ballistic, telling the men to go fuck themselves. Now people disagree with me, but I think it was those bikers."

John stared at her, intrigued by the story. He eagerly listened as she went on.

"They said his days were numbered, then left. Two hours later three members from Gutter Street Mafia showed up with masks on their faces. They got into a shouting match with

Priest and his cronies. Two Punks in ski masks pulled out guns. Charlie was coming out of the motel to go for a walk, and he got caught in the crossfire."

"Which one of them shot him?" he asked without looking at her.

She rubbed her eyes with a sweaty hand. "I don't know, it was too dark to see. The street light above them got blown out, it all happened so fast."

John leaned back in his seat and closed his eyes. Her words were like a slap in the face. The fact that his friend was gunned down by some low-life puke was too much to bear.

"Were you in the Army?" April stared at the dog tags around his neck.

"Yeah." He closed his eyes again and nodded. "Me and Charlie served together. I got wounded in action and poisoned with radiation, so they let me go early."

"Oh." Her voice dropped to a low pitch. "I'm sorry to hear that. I know it must be tough, being out of work and all."

He shrugged, the expression on his face indifferent. "Not really. The Army gave me benefits for the rest of my life. Even if I don't work right away, I'm straight."

John knew deep down that what he was saying was bullshit. Sure the benefits were nice, but he was a soldier. He didn't care about getting money for the rest of his life, he wanted to be active again. When the government told him that he couldn't serve anymore it had crushed him. He couldn't see himself at some boring desk job, being a combat soldier was what he was born to do.

Speaking of combat...

He rubbed the side of his head to see if it was still bleeding. "I need to get to the hospital and get checked. Real *quick*."

"Checked out for what?" she asked, puzzled.

"Are you kidding me? That Priest asshole knocked the shit out of me. I know I'm going to need stitches for this.

Probably have a huge gash in my head."

He stared at April, and recognized the look on her face all too well. It was the same look the doctors at Walter Reed had given him when he'd told them about his nightmares in those grueling therapy sessions. It was even the same look his own mother gave him when he went back home to visit her after the war. It was that *You've gone crazy* look, one that he'd grown to hate.

"John," she said, her eyes steady, "there is no gash in your head."

He touched the side of his head again and looked down at his palm. No blood. There was a bench across from them with a mirror on it. He went over and snatched the mirror up, glancing at it. Sure enough, his head was fine. But he remembered feeling the gash, even felt the chunk of flesh being knocked away when Priest clubbed him with that cursed aluminum bat.

But how is that possible?

Perplexed, he sat the mirror back on the bench and held onto the rail for awhile. He stared out of the window, not sure what to make of what he saw. Maybe he'd been wrong. Maybe he didn't get hit with a bat after all and he'd just imagined the whole thing. John knew how the mind could play tricks on a person when they were under stress. Hell, he'd been through combat plenty of times to know that for himself.

But deep down in his heart he knew this was different. That punk rock goon *did* hit him with a bat, he'd felt the blow, and there was no getting around that little fact at all, no matter what kind of idea he wanted to cook up in his head.

"So why were those…Punk guys trying to hurt you back there?" he asked, trying to change the subject.

"Because I was there when Charlie got shot." She shifted on the bench uncomfortably. "I don't know who pulled the trigger, but I heard the guy's voice. I'll never forget that deep, frog-sounding voice as long as I live. It sounded like broken glass being ground up in his throat."

He cocked his head to the side as he continued to stare out the window. "So it could've been Priest? Or these Gutter Street guys?"

"I don't know John," she said, not trying to hide the irritation in her voice. "It was dark, okay? It could've been either one of them. I'm sorry about your friend."

April said something else to him, but he didn't hear it. His mind was a thousand miles away. He was back in the jungles of Brazil, fighting against Falcon. A memory of the enemy capturing him and holding him hostage popped in his head.

A couple of Falcon soldiers had him and one of his infantry buddies tied up. They Peeled the skin off of his poor friend, then poured salt and vinegar all over his body. While three of the enemies were doing this, a fourth one came over to John, and doused him in water. The man had huge, ugly, purple bumps on his face that looked like they would explode liquid at any time. The repulsive soldier grabbed an electric cable and had zapped his chest with it, causing him to shake violently. John felt like his whole body would burst, and was surprised that it hadn't. He'd clenched with each dreadful zap, praying for death the whole time. To make things worse, the Falcon men had took his buddy and threw him in a wooden tub filled with dwarf rats. He watched in horror as the fierce rodents chomped into his flesh. One of them took a greedy chunk out of his throat, exposing glistening muscle and his naked Adam's apple. His screams turned into bubbling cries as they ripped him apart. Within seconds they swarmed him, and he disappeared entirely as the furry fucks tore him to bloody pieces.

That invidious memory had haunted John for months on end, and eventually plagued his dreams. Some nights after the war he'd have horrible nightmares about those rats eating his friend. Except in his dreams, the rats had human faces. In some of his dreams the Falcon soldiers were actually goblins, and they had tentacles with claws, chasing him around the horrid jungles that was thousands of miles away from his home.

One dream in particular he'd remembered was the worse of all. A man with the head of a Cicada would chase him. The Cicada man would tear his own flesh away, ripping chunks of his bloody body and eating it as he ran towards him. As John would try to get away hands would reach up from the ground, and pull him through the earth as goat man pursued him. Hot fingers would tear into his body, burning him to the bone.

He shuddered at the memory, and tried to put it out of his head. No use in thinking about it now because he would most likely be dreaming about it tonight. It got to the point where he hated going to sleep, fearing that the goddamn nightmares would return. The Ambien the doctors gave him didn't do jack, so after awhile he'd just stopped taking it. Therapy wasn't helping. Nothing was helping. And forget talking to friends. He'd found out that when he'd came back from the war they were coming by less and less, then eventually stopped coming around altogether.

The subway train came to a screeching halt, and the doors opened. Fresh adrenaline leaked into John's veins. Something was wrong. As they walked off the train car and stepped out into the tunnels, every hair on the back of his neck stood. He'd gotten this same feeling when Falcon had ambushed him.

"Stay close to me," he whispered.

"What's wro—"

His eyes narrowed to slits. "I said stay close, *dammit!*"

She flinched at the sound of his voice. Feeling anxious she glanced around, wondering why he was so irritated.

Whatever had him spooked was starting to freak her out.

The buzzing lights above them swung in the subway tunnels, the newspapers blowing in the wind as the train sped off. The dripping sound of a leaky water faucet from a distant bathroom echoed in the tunnels. Each footstep they took seemed to magnify a thousand times louder than what they should have been. Something was wrong. Terribly wrong.

They hurried forward. Heavy footsteps echoed in the shadows. John balled his fists up, his internal alarms going off like bombs. A second set of footsteps followed. Then another set. A tall man with a piercing green eye and dreadlocks emerged from the shadows. He noticed that the man was missing his left eye, and that there was a gaping black hole in the socket of where it should've been.

The dreaded man had a full beard that was un-kept, adding to his fierce appearance. A scar ran from his left ear to the left side of his nose, and the face of a red lion was tattooed on his right arm. A green vest covered his bare chest, and a military belt held up his green camouflage pants. A long, shiny machete was in his right hand.

"Holy shit," April whispered under her breath. "King Eddie."

King Eddie took slow, calculated steps towards them, the echoing sound of his boots bouncing off the walls. He stopped and stood about a hundred feet away from them. He spat on the floor and raised his machete towards the ceiling.

"Ya bout' dead tonight, boy!"

The sound of his thick Jamaican accent reverberated inside of the tunnels. Right after he made his threat, two of his dreadlocked henchmen stepped out of the shadows with M-16s. They didn't hesitate.

John grabbed April and took her to the floor as King Eddie's posse opened up on them with a hail of gunfire. Bullets chipped away at the floors and walls around them. He covered her as they moved closer, firing madly in the

KingStreet tunnels.

"Turn dem now same they turn to me, no?" Eddie moved forward as well, howling his insults. "Fuck dem Ras clot!"

The bullets were getting too close for comfort. Lucky for them, King Eddie's men couldn't shoot for shit, but that didn't mean that they wouldn't be mowed down eventually. John got off of April and took a chance. He rolled forward and came to his feet, dashing toward the gunmen. Gaining speed he leaped in the air and kicked one of the gunners in their torso. The man dropped his rifle and collapsed, clutching his chest.

John jumped up and did a knee drop on the man's head, knocking him completely out. The other posse member aimed at him and squeezed the trigger, his gun clicking dry. He fished a fresh magazine out of his camo pants and fumbled with it as he tried to reload his gun. John zeroed in on him and grabbed the weapon. They struggled with the gun as Eddie moved past them.

April rolled on her back and got to her knee. A giant shadow cast over her. She glanced up to see King Eddie towering over her. He twisted the left side of his face up, forming a sickening grin. Raising the blade high above his head, he nodded to her slowly.

"Execution style, bitch."

He swung it down violently. She dove forward and tackled him by the waist, making him miss. April let go and bent down, grabbing him behind his legs. In one fluid motion she scooped him up and dropped him to the floor. He lost his machete, a surprised look plastered on his face. Eddie cocked his free leg back and kicked her in the face, sending her flying.

John managed to wrestle the M-16 away from the sturdy henchman. He smashed the butt of the gun into his face until he laid unconscious. He turned around to see Eddie on the ground, reaching for his machete. April was laying on the subway tracks, clutching the side of her face. Fear hit him when he heard a familiar sound. The sound of a train coming.

"April!" He dropped the gun and bolted towards the tracks. "April get outta there!"

Hot, searing pain erupted from his chest, and he realized that King Eddie had sliced him. He swung his blade, trying to hack him into pieces. John panicked and dodged the attacks, knowing that he was fighting him to keep from rescuing her. He side-stepped the tall goon and punched him in his sternum, knocking the wind out of him.

Eddie crumpled to the floor. John rushed over to where the tracks were and slid to the edge. The train was close and it would reach them at any moment, flattening April into a pancake. He hopped down on the tracks and grabbed her arm, slinging her over his back. With all his strength he hurled her up to safety on the floor above.

John leaped out of the hole. A second later the train roared past him, the gush of air blowing his bloody shirt in the wind. If he would've blinked, he'd be dead. He rushed to April and knelt down beside her, checking her neck for a pulse. *Thank God* he thought. That had been too close!

"Mmm…oooh, my head…"

April blinked her eyes open. There was going to be a nasty bruise on the side of her face, but she'd live. John glanced around and saw that the two goons were still knocked out. King Eddie was no where in sight.

"Hey." He gently shook her. "Hey wake up."

"John? Wha…where's Eddie?"

He helped her up. "Don't worry about that right now. We gotta get out of here and to your place. It's not safe here."

John put her arm around his neck and grabbed her by the waist, escorting her to the end of the tunnel where the stairs were.

FIVE

APRIL'S APARTMENT WAS SURPRISINGLY immaculate, despite the fact that the Summerville Heights area was a real shit hole. John came to the conclusion that much of BayView City was a dump, and so far none of what he'd seen had proven him wrong. The only difference between KingStreet and this place was that Montebello was more run-down.

The building she lived in was falling apart, and there were curb creatures roaming around outside. Still, she'd managed to keep her place up, it was like stepping into another world when she'd let him in. A cream-colored Persian rug covered the brown floors. The walls were painted ivory, the pictures of her family hung up on them. Her kitchen was small but clean. Not a dirty pot or pan in sight. Her bedroom was way in the back, and an antique coffee table was in the small living room.

A Zenith TV was perched on a wooden cabinet, and at first glance, John was sure that it would crash under the weight of the old model. He sat on her burgundy couch in the living room, taking in the pleasant surroundings. Despite the fact that her apartment complex smelled like human feces, *her* place had a pleasant aroma. On her kitchen counter was a plug-in pot full of potpourri, the smell of strawberries and flowers filling the air.

Yup. This is definitely a woman's apartment.

"John! Come here, I want to show you something."

He got up and went to the back where her bedroom was. He stepped in and saw her sitting at a desk in front of a sleek-looking computer. She stood up and motioned him to sit down, handing him a stack of papers with pictures on them.

"What's this?"

She brushed her hair away from her face and leaned over his shoulder, pointing at the first page. "This is a list of all the violent criminals in BayView."

They were mug shots. Wanted posters of the creeps. Intrigued, he flipped through the pages. Maybe there were some clues that could tell him what the hell was going on, and lead him to Charlie's murderer.

```
                    WANTED
Michael Priest
Street Name: Priest
Height: 6 ft 4"
Weight: 200 lbs
Eye Color: Blue
Hair Color: Yellow Mohawk
Scars: Scar over left eye
Tattoos: ARK on both hands
Hometown: Los Angeles, CA

                  DESCRIPTION
Joined a street gang back in L.A. and
robbed a liquor store at the age of
thirteen. Arrested for possession of
narcotics and intent to distribute. Robbed
another liquor store at age eighteen with
an aluminum bat, beating the store owner
severely. Escaped from prison and fled to
BayView City. Started up the gang Anarchy
on KingStreet and took over the area.
Suspect is considered to be armed and
dangerous.

                    WANTED
EDDIE SEAGA
Street Name: King Eddie
```

```
Height: 6 ft 3"
Weight: 190 lbs
Eyes: Green, left-eye is missing
Hair: Black, long dreadlocks, full beard
Scars: Horizontal scar on left side of
face
Tattoos: Face of a red lion on right arm
Hometown: Kingston, Jamaica
```

```
                DESCRIPTION
Leader of a notorious street gang in
Jamaica for 20 years. Fled to America and
hid in BayView City. Started the
KingStreet Posse and is at war with
Anarchy and Gutter Street. Currently runs
the KingStreet Tunnels. If you see this
man do not approach him, notify
authorities immediately. Suspect is to be
considered armed and dangerous.
```

John leaned back in his seat while he read the descriptions. As he scanned the other reports, April kept babbling on about Lang's safety, and how the hoodlums should be taken off the streets.

"Look," she said, "those scumbags are intimidating him! One day these men with masks busted into the Sun Tree with bats. They said he had to pay them protection money. I knew it was Anarchy, so I called the police! But the fucking cops came right to my apartment and asked me for a statement. So as you might have guessed the goddamn gangs found out I told on them, and now you know why I have to—"

John ignored her and read the rest of the wanted posters.

```
                  WANTED
GARY WASHINGTON
Street Name: GUNS
```

```
Height: 5 ft 11"
Weight: 165 lbs
Eyes: Dark Brown
Hair: Black cornrows
Scars: Right eye is smaller and bruised
from fighting
Tattoos: None
Hometown: Unknown

           DESCRIPTION
Not much is known about Washington.
Arrested for fighting in the Town Hall Bar
a week ago. Currently a murder suspect in
the shooting of two Punks, five Posse
members, and one of his own associates
named Q. He is a fugitive, and considered
armed and—
```

    John's head was spinning by the time he'd finished reading the papers. He let them drop to his lap and sat quietly as April complained how she wanted to help her friend, and get out of the city. Which one of these assholes was responsible for Charlie's death? Was it the Punks or the bikers? Judging from the way the gangs were shooting in the streets today, he wouldn't have been surprised if both sides were responsible for killing him, but somehow he doubted.

    "How'd you get a hold of all this?" John turned and faced her.

    She stared at him and grinned. "I hacked into the police's database. Not that hard to tell you the truth."

    He nodded slowly. "Listen, I appreciate all of your help. If you want to leave the city, that's up to you. To tell you the truth, I don't blame you, it ain't safe to stay here. But I'm staying."

    "For how long?"

    He rubbed his chin and stared blankly at the computer screen. "Until I find Charlie's killers."

"There's blood on your shirt."

John snapped out of his daze and turned away from the screen. He stared up at her. "What's that?"

"You've got blood on your shirt." She pointed to the huge, diagonal-red stain. "Is—is that your blood? Or someone else's?"

In a flash he remembered how King Eddie slashed him under the tunnels. An icy feeling traveled down his spine with invisible fingers, making him tremble. So much adrenaline had pumped through him during the fight that he'd forgotten he'd been cut. What amazed him more was that he didn't feel any pain now. He stood up and slowly pulled his shirt off, preparing himself for the worst. Now he was sure he was going to die.

"Oh, God!" April winced and covered her mouth. "How did you get someone else's blood on you like that!"

John gathered up enough nerve to look down at his chest. Puzzled, he wondered why there wasn't a gushing wound where the blade had pierced him. He wasn't happy that he was alright, and didn't know what upset him more; not dying from his injuries, or why he healed from injuries that could kill any normal human being. He didn't like this. At all.

"What's that?" she asked, pointing to his right shoulder.

John rubbed his shoulder. "It's a tattoo of Jesus Christ's face. Got it when I was stationed in Brazil."

"Wow, it's really nice. Looks like it took a long time, too. Did it hurt?"

"Nah. It stung for the first minute, but I got used to it after awhile."

She frowned again. "Is that more blood?"

He glanced down. "Yeah. I'm fine, though."

"Well just be thankful it's not yours," April said, taking the red-stained t-shirt from him. She pointed to the bathroom behind her on the right side of the bed. "Why don't you go in there and clean yourself up? There's fresh towels on the third shelf to the right, and I think there's some clean shirts under the bathroom sink. My brother visited me last month and he left a lot of his stuff here."

John's mind was going in a million directions. He couldn't make any sense of what was happening. Had he slipped into another dimension where cuts and bruises heal themselves in mere hours? Or was this just more symptoms of PTS? Maybe he'd just hallucinated the whole thing, and never got bludgeoned or cut up in the first place. It wasn't the first time his mind had tricked him.

"When you're done in the shower just make yourself at home." She walked out of the bedroom, talking as she went. "There's food in the fridge if your hungry, and..."

He didn't hear the rest. He closed the door behind him and undressed. He hopped in the shower and turned the dial on, letting the warm water beat across his shoulders. Closing his eyes, he wondered if the radiation poisoning could have altered his body somehow, making him able to heal faster than any normal person on earth.

Great. So now I'm some kind of fucking wolverine from a comic book, all I need are the claws. Come on John, *get a hold of yourself.*

He washed the lather of soap off his body, then turned the dial to off. Pushing the curtains aside he stepped out of the shower, and went to the cabinet with the fresh towels. After drying himself he wrapped the white towel around his body, and opened the cabinet under the sink. A dozen of Haines t-shirts were neatly folded inside, just like she'd said they would be. Next to the shirts and other feminine products, John spotted a pair of creased up khakis that her brother had left behind as well. He reached down and pulled them out, hoping they would fit. No such luck, judging by the way they looked.

Tink, tink, tink!

An old fashioned switch blade fell out of the pants

pocket. He held them up a second, frowning.

He neatly placed the pants back under the sink the way he'd found them, and picked up the blade. It had a dark jade handle, clearly an antique. He stared at himself in the mirror for a moment and rubbed the area of his chest that had been cut. He glanced at the switchblade again, then formed an idea in his head.

John took a deep breath and pressed the handle of the knife, making the blade appear. His heart raced as he turned it towards him. After a few tense seconds he mustered up what little nerves he had left, and stabbed himself in the chest.

"Ahhh!"

He immediately regretted his actions. *That shit hurt!* Fresh red blood gushed from the right side of his chest as he yanked the blade out. It poured out of him, dotting the sink and dark-pink rugs that covered the white tiles. He covered his chest, the blood oozing between his fingers. Taking his hand away he stepped up to the mirror and examined himself. His stomach turned when he saw that the gaping knife wound where he'd stabbed himself begin to close up by itself.

"John?"

He flinched at the sound of her voice.

"Are you alright in there?"

He touched the part of his chest where the hole used to be. Healed. Completely healed and closed up, as if he'd never even stuck himself. He scooped up the bloody knife from the floor, and began slicing his left forearm with it. He stabbed himself in the stomach, then glanced at the mirror, horrified by what he saw.

Again, the blood had seeped from his cuts, then his wounds closed in mere seconds. This wasn't an hallucination, it was real. A little too real for him.

What the hell is happening to me?

"John?"

He blinked and turned the water faucet on, rinsing the

blade off. "Uh, yeah! I'm okay! Just slipped in the shower!"

He yanked the towel from around his body and soaked part of it in water. He wiped the sink and floors where the blood had leaked. He bawled the towel up and threw it in the sky-blue waste basket next to the toilet, then wiped the switchblade dry, and placed it back inside the khakis.

He quickly dressed himself in the Levis' he'd worn earlier, and threw a fresh T on. He steadied his trembling hands and fumbled with the door, careful to keep his emotions in check. April had entered the room with a fresh pair of socks.

"Here you go. He left these, too."

He forced a smile and took the socks, trying to avoid eye contact with her as he moved past her and headed for the doorway. She followed him out as he sat on the couch. As she spoke he put both of his hands on his jeans and squeezed his knees, and tried very hard not to lose his fucking mind.

He turned away from the sunlight pouring through the window. Turning away wasn't helping, so he covered his face with his hands.

"Listen I'm sorry, but you're going to have to sleep on the couch tonight," April said.

"No problem." He felt a soft hand touch his shoulder.

"Thank you again for saving my life."

He didn't answer her. He was too busy being terrified by what he'd saw. What had happened to him over there in the jungle? Had the radiation really done this to him? That was the only explanation that he could come up with. Nothing else made sense.

"John? John!"

He took his hands away from his face. It was dark outside, and he noticed that she was standing in front of him. Confused, he searched her hazel eyes for answers.

"What happened?"

She smoothed her hair back with both hands. "You fell

asleep, guy. You looked so peaceful that I didn't want to wake you, so I took a shower and went to the clothing store. Here, I bought you some extra boxers."

"Thank you," he said, closing his eyes and shaking his head as he took them, "but you really didn't have to."

He noticed that she'd changed into a purple shirt and tight jean shorts. The moonlight shone through the window, illuminating her sun-tanned skin, showing off her curvy figure. Sweat spotted her upper lip, and ran down her chin all the way to her neck.

She held up something bloody in her hand. "What happened to my towel?"

He darted his eyes from left to right, cooking up something to say to her. "Oh. Well, some of the blood had leaked down into my pants, and it dried on my legs. I had to wipe it off, you know."

She nodded, her facial expression softening. "I'm going to call Mr. Lang and see if he's alright. Try to get some sleep, okay?"

"Thanks," he said, nodding slightly at her, "I think I will."

April flashed her sunshine smile, then turned and moved back to her bedroom, disappearing into the darkness. She closed the door and a yellow light flashed under it. John tilted his head back on the soft couch and closed his eyes, trying to doze again.

SIX

"FUCK YOU!"

John yelled at the Falcon Soldiers behind him. He turned and shot them with his rifle...but they wouldn't die. The bullets slammed into their heads but they wouldn't die. He blew a soldier's head apart and watched his brains spill out of his face.

The soldier didn't go down. He picked up part of his brain and kept running, chasing him through the blazing jungle. John shot another one, blowing his arm completely off. The man laughed, ignoring his missing limb and the blood pumping from his body.

He squeezed the trigger, blasting the enemy away. They kept rising. Heads and legs were being shot off. No matter how badly he hurt them they kept coming. They wouldn't stop.

Headless men rose from the ground, chasing him, stretching their bloody arms towards him. Falcon men crawled after him, their guts spilling out of their bodies.

Click, click!

"Shit!"

John glared at his empty rifle. He reached inside his vest and grabbed another magazine. He slapped it in, then spun and fired at the undying soldiers...and panicked when he saw that one of them had the head of a goat.

He squeezed the trigger and blew the goat-soldier's head off. The headless soldier reached his arms out, stretching them forward. His arms grew long, turning rubbery and snake-like, reaching until they were ten feet. Suddenly they were fifteen feet long...twenty feet long.

Jesus Christ, why won't they die?

Hundreds of them were after him now. Their screams turned to laughter. Their laughter turned to howling, their howling changed to warpness, something he couldn't recognize, but he knew the sounds were evil.

Sprinting faster he took out a grenade. He pulled the pin and tossed it behind him, hoping it would destroy them. Tree branches smacked his face and went by him in a blur.

A loud explosion rocked the jungle floor. Screaming filled the air as he felt the heat from the blast. He kept booking, the only thought in his mind was reaching the chopper.

But I don't see the chopper! Where the hell are they?

Everybody was dead. Charlie, Skip, Chako. They'd been killed in the ambush, he was the only one left. Before Chako died he'd managed to raise them on his radio—

—and then a flash grenade fell from the sky, blowing him in half.

John watched as the grenade turned him into a cloud of red mist. He'd watched in horror as Keith's guts spilled out of his body. He'd tried to help Keith put his intestines back inside, but it was useless.

John stopped running and spun around. Burning trees and black smoke were the only things he could see. *Did I finally get them?* he thought as he clutched his gun. Seconds of silence passed.

"Yaaagh!"

Skeleton soldiers emerged from the smoke. They barreled towards him, screaming for his blood.

He ran, pumping his arms wildly, tearing through the chaotic jungle. He dropped his M-16 and hopped over a dead Army soldier, unable to recognize the charred face. Suddenly the demonic noises behind him stopped.

He came to a clearing and stood, afraid to turn around. When he did he was relieved to see that they were gone.

Suddenly his arm felt tingly.

Confused, he stood in the clearing. He glanced down at his arm, not liking what was happening. The tingling sensation spread throughout his body. It felt like a thousand fingers were crawling under his skin, the creeping sensation numbing him.

"What's...happening to meee!"

The blue sky turned crimson. Thunder rumbled from above, and green drops rained down. The rain touched his face, burning his skin. His fingers turned to liquid and his body began to melt like burned wax.

"Argh!"

John sat up from the couch and cried out. He glanced around frantically, realizing that he wasn't in the jungle.

Another FUCKING nightmare!

He cursed himself, hoping he didn't wake April. He waited for her to open the door and come out of her room. But she didn't. She was sleeping soundly in her bed.

He laid back down and knew he wasn't going to get any sleep.

A full hour had passed by and he was still wide awake. His eyes jutted open and he sat in the darkness, gazing into the brilliant white moon that stared back at him from outside.

Satisfied that she was still asleep John tip-toed towards the window. He lifted it up as quietly as he could, sneaking out into the dangerous night.

SEVEN

MICHAEL PRIEST TOOK ANOTHER HIT OF COCAINE in the abandoned warehouse. Glassy-eyed and amped up he gazed around at his fellow Punks. The whole gang was there, some of them sitting on beat up, busted couches. Others were standing against the wall or leaning on cracked-up furniture, taking hits of powder and drinking strong alcohol. He snorted a few more lines off of a cracked mirror, then zeroed in on one of the Punks on the couch.

Priest ran up on Scotty, a twenty-year-old with a baby face who looked more like he was a kid. The other goons scattered, getting out of his way as he got in the younger man's face. Scotty was asleep because of drinking and taking too many downers, but he was about to get a rude awakening.

"Scotty," Priest said, his voice low and distant sounding, "why the fuck are you asleep, Scotty. It's a party, Scotty. Wake the fuck up."

Some of the others were laughing because they knew what was coming next. Priest was a raving mad man whenever he was hopped up, and he loved to bully whoever he damned well pleased. The young man, as always, just happened to be his favorite target.

"Scotty, I'm going to slap you in two-point *five* seconds. Prepare yourself!" He raised his hand high in the air, his gargantuan palm facing the ceiling, and brought it down hard across his face.

Whack!

The room erupted in laughter, the animal-like goons besides themselves from watching the ritual-like show. The young man's green eyes jerked open, the surprise on his face fueling the antics. Yes, it was going to be another humiliating night for him.

"Wake your fucking ass up Scotty…it's a party! It's a party, and everyone is invited! Everyone is invited!" He grabbed the man by the collar of his t-shirt. "And all are welcome."

Scotty tried to fight him off, throwing uppercuts, but of course, his efforts were useless. He grabbed his hand and put it behind his back, lifted him off the couch, then wrapped his arm around his neck, choking the life out of him.

"Get off me!" Scotty's face was turning red, changing the color of dark-blue in seconds. "Priest I can't… *breeeathe.*"

His malicious grin widened, and a deep frown formed on his forehead. "Scotty, I will break your fucking neck."

Bugg, an older Punk around Priest's age, was the only one in the room who wasn't laughing. Out of the entire gang he was the most level-headed. He hated when he got like this, seemed like every time he had to wind up pulling him off of someone. He ran over and yanked him away.

"Priest," Bugg said, his deep voice rising, "get a grip man. You're killing him!"

Priest faced him. "Dude—Scotty's my friend, dude. He *needs* this!"

Amazingly enough, his voice turned logical, and even sounded heart-felt and genuine. The young man collapsed back onto the couch, gasping for air. Priest pushed Bugg away, then got at him again.

"Scotty—I'm going to slap you in three point *five* seconds. One…two…"

Whack!

Again, the mindless hooligans around them roared. Tears welled up in the man's eyes, his face burning red from the slaps. In a sudden rage he dove into Priest, spearing him. And again, his efforts were futile. Priest kneed him in the chest, knocking the wind out of him, then punched him in the back of the head, mashing his green mohawk. He threw him back on the couch. Bugg grabbed him again.

"What are you doing, man?" Bugg yelled at the top of his lungs. "Chill the fuck out!"

Priest snatched his hand out of his grip, then raised his fist in the air. He locked him in a mean stare. "Dude, I will break your fucking nose."

Bugg backed off, and Priest left through the door-less entrance. Silence. At long last. But not for long. He stormed back into the hide-out.

"Scotty...who started the Korean War conflict?" He made straight towards him again, stopping right in front of the couch. He balled up both of his fists, ready to pummel him into a young, bloody pulp.

Bugg blocked his path, making himself a human shield. "Dude, you're losing it man. Come on knock this shit off!"

Priest shoved him roughly. There was no reasoning in his eyes at all. Only madness. He turned towards the crowd of goons behind him.

"I can do a back-flip...in three-point-five *seconds*."

"Priest!"

Bugg was fed up. He grabbed hold of Priest's shoulders, trying to calm him down from his high. There was no use trying to compromise. The man had gone absolutely bat crazy, his wide, pupil-dilated eyes darting around like a rabid dog's.

"Priest, come on, man!"

"Bugg. Are you on a roll? Are you on a roll, dog? You wanna be a combat ninja?" Priest shrugged his hand away, then cocked his fist back.

He punched Bugg to the ground, slapped Scotty a few more times, then dove behind the ripped yellow-and-green couch. When he came up, his aluminum bat was in his hands. As if on cue, the others scrambled in different directions.

"Yaaargh!"

Priest charged at everyone, trying to knock the first person he saw in the head. He spun around in wild circles, the bat stretched out before him at arms length, knocking over tables and beer bottles. Scotty watched in horror as his bat-shit leader continued his psychotic rampage. Bugg was on the ground, knocked out cold.

Amidst the chaos, Scotty saw his chance. He leaped off of the couch and made for the door as the others ducked and dodged out of the mad man's way. Bolting out of the doorway he hit the street and took off, vowing never to return again.

After a few minutes that seemed like forever, the insanity died down. Priest commanded everyone to circle around him. He raised his bat high.

"We're gonna get those bikers!" His voice rasped with an intensity of a preacher. "And Gutter Street Mafia! You hear me? We're gonna get em' all! No matter *what*!"

Cheers followed as the mighty Anarchy Crew jumped around with sticks and weapons, ready to kill any enemy on sight.

EIGHT

A MILLION THOUGHTS RACED THROUGH JOHN'S head as he moved down the cracked, broken streets of the city. He was still far from KingStreet and sped up the pace, wanting to get there as soon as possible. This was a part of the city he'd never seen before; across the street to his left was a long strip mall of buildings and bootleg clothing stores. Inside of the windows he saw cheap shirts hung up, and knew from the looks of the fabric that they'd been made in a factory, then had a fake logo of well-known brand names sewn on.

Broken whiskey bottles and crushed beer cans littered the lengthy sidewalks. In front of him, newspapers laid on the ground. A pack of mangy dogs were tearing away at tossed food from an overturned trashcan in an alley. He tensed a little when he saw them, then kept it cool and moved on. The vicious mutts were too concerned with eating rotten garbage to even think about bothering him. He walked a few blocks more, and stopped in front of a brick building that appeared to have been bombed out. The red bricks and broken windows were charred with old smoke.

Flick!

John tensed when he saw a shadowy figure with a gold cigarette lighter leaning against the brick wall. The yellow flame showed a bearded man with black sunglasses. As he moved closer to the man, he noticed that he was built like a fire truck. He also noticed that what the man was smoking was not a cigarette.

How long has he been standing there, for Christ's sakes? I didn't even see him!

That familiar, rotten herb smell filled his nostrils when he stopped and stood fifteen feet away from him. John balled his fists and sized the man up; he was well over six-feet tall, and looked to be around two-hundred-and-sixty pounds of pure terror. He had a full head of gray hair that was slicked back, and braided into a long pony tail that went all the way down to the back of his blue-sleeveless jacket. A thin, gold cross hanging from a chain rested against his white t-shirt, and his blue jeans were rolled up at the bottom, covering black boots that looked like they were used for stomping someone out. He squared off, ready for anything this smoking giant might have up his sleeve.

"Take it easy kid," the man said, gazing down at the sidewalk, "I'm not going to hurt you."

John squinted his eyes and shook his head a little. *Who the fuck is this guy to tell me to take it easy?* he thought. He took it as an insult. The large biker stepped away from the wall and moved towards him, shoving his gold lighter inside of his pocket. No doubt about it, he was intimidating. Just the size of him would even make Frankenstein shit his pants.

"I heard you've been causing quite a ruckus in this city." The biker took another drag of what he was smoking on as he sized John up. "Kinda' surprises me. A little runt like you should be at home with his mommy."

John unclenched his fists, but still kept his feet planted. "And who are you supposed to be?"

"What are you about, a buck fifty?" The man flat-out ignored his question.

"I said who *are* you?"

The man stared at him a moment, his face stone and expressionless. After a few uncomfortable seconds of silence he took another drag, blew a large cloud of smoke into the air, then nodded his head.

"The name's Gus. I run Vegas Ave." With his freehand he made a circling gesture towards the surrounding area.

"What's your name kid?"

"John," he said, his voice dripping with enmity, "and I'm not a *kid*."

Gus gestured towards the dark alley where the brick building was. "Follow me, kid. Let's have a talk."

He took a few steps towards the alley, then stopped and turned around, noticing that John hadn't budged. He saw the unease in his face, and understood completely. It was obvious that the young man had some trust issues with him.

"Listen kid," he called out in a calm voice, "if I wanted to hurt you, then I woulda' done it already. Now follow me."

John developed a strong dislike for the local gang life in this city. Since he'd gotten to the Bay he'd been beaten, stabbed, and mashed in the head by hooligans. As far as he was concerned the bikers were no better than any of the other punks. But there was something different about Gus. He was obviously on the other side of the law, but he didn't get the same vibe from him that he'd gotten from the other scum. He was clearly an asshole, but he seemed genuine about not hurting him. He sighed, then followed the smoking thug into the alley.

He's not with those other bikers who brawled the Punks earlier. But is he savage like them? I wonder.

Gus adjusted his sunglasses as they walked. "Kid you're in big trouble. Word on the street is that you've got a price on your head. Nobody knows your name, but they know who you are. You know that Priest is after you, right?"

"Is that a fact?" He gazed at the ground as they walked.

"Yeah. That's a fact. Priest is not exactly someone you want to mess with. Neither is Guns. What I'm confused about is why you have a death wish."

"A few days ago my friend Charlie was gunned down in this city, and I'm trying to find out who pulled the trigger. Priest or Guns. I'm going to find out which one of them was responsible, hunt that person down, and kill them. And no one is going to stop me."

"I heard about that shooting." Gus turned and faced him, offering him a hit. John shook his head, and they continued down the alley. "Well, that sucks what they did to your friend, but you're clearly not in any position to do anything about it. Going up against them is a suicide mission."

John heard the feint sound of rock music up ahead. It got louder and louder as they moved on, and after a few minutes of walking in silence, he could see the source of the blaring music. There was a bar up ahead with a red, neon sign that read Torchy's, and from the looks of it, he could tell it wasn't his kind of place. Out front on the wooden steps were a hand full of bikers dressed like Gus. They waved at him and raised their beer bottles in the air.

"Sounds pretty stupid to me," Gus said, ignoring the bikers greetings. "If you're stupid enough to go up against those two, then that's you're problem kid."

"Maybe so," John said, "but that's none of you're business in the first place. So worry about your own problems, and let me do me."

They stopped walking and looked at each other. Gus took his sunglasses off and stared at him with his slate, blue eyes, locking him into a fierce stare. John met his gaze evenly, not backing down from his stare. After a few tense seconds, Gus smiled at him.

"Alright. Fair enough." His smile faded, and his face turned gravely serious. He stepped toward him. "But know this. Do trouble if you want, but don't bring trouble around here. This is the Ave, and the last person who tried to walk in here looking for trouble, didn't walk out again."

There was nothing John could say. Even though Gus was different from the other crews in the area, he was clearly not the one to mess with. He was positive that without his newly gained powers, he'd be no match for Gus in a physical confrontation.

Maybe not even with *my powers. This guy could bench press a whole house by himself.*

"What about Guns and his crew?" John frowned.

Gus looked him square in his eyes and broke out in a smile. "He doesn't fuck with us. He knows better than to come around here."

The doors to Torchy's swung open, and out stepped two voluptuous women. The tall lady with the red dress had heavy thighs and smooth legs. Her curly hair flowed down to her back, and she stared lustfully at Gus with piercing, green eyes. The other woman had a blue dress on, and she brushed strands of her long, blonde hair away from her blue eyes. Various tattoos covered her left leg and ran up her huge thigh. Both women walked over to Gus and clung to his waist.

"So long John," Gus said. "You should come by sometime. If you live that long."

Gus put his arms around the young women, and the three of them turned away from John and started for Torchy's. He went his own way, focusing back on his mission.

NINE

JOHN CREPT UP TO THE ABANDONED
warehouse, hidden by the blanket of darkness. He climbed up a sturdy drainpipe, topped the roof, and hid behind a bulky fan unit. One of Priest's thugs was in front of a set of windows, standing guard, gazing out into the streets for any sign of gang invasion.

    He snuck up on the Punk and put him in a sleeper move. Gasping for air and flailing his arms wildly he struggled for a few seconds, then closed his eyes and lost consciousness. John gently laid him on the ground and peered through one of the dirty windows. Something was happening inside. Priest was apparently going out of his ever-loving mind, smacking some young kid around.

    He watched in disgust as they went wild inside, jumping around like a bunch of crazed zoo animals, screaming and shouting. Surveying the area inside, he tried to do a mental head-count of how many thugs there were, and how in the hell he was going to get to the leader.

    I'm one-hundred percent sure that Priest killed Charlie. But how am I gonna get to him? I'll be torn to pieces before I can get six feet to him. There has to be another way...

"Hey asshole! Bring your crew outside!"

Out of nowhere Gary Washington and his gang assembled in the street. They had the building surrounded. Knives, sticks, and guns were clutched in their hands, and they were ready to tear Anarchy a new one. The Punks ran to the front door and windows like angry hornets, grabbing sticks, bats, bricks, pipes, and broken glass bottles.

"Get those motherfuckers!" Priest rose his bat to the sky and pumped his other fist up.

On his command the mohawked murderers stormed out, clashing with Gary and his crew. The war brewed in the streets, fists and weapons flying. John gently opened one of the ceiling windows and slid inside, scaling his way into the moldy-smelling warehouse. Using his army training he took extra care not to make a sound as his feet touched the stairs.

"Kill Guns!" a random thug yelled.

Priest was searching one of the boxes for something, no doubt another weapon. He reached inside of one, smiled, and pulled out a hand grenade. Stuffing it inside of his leather jacket he paused for a moment, then turned around. He was greeted by a brown fist.

Stunned, he fell backwards to the floor. He shook his head from side to side, still holding on to his deadly bat. He glared up at his attacker.

"You, you're that same asshole from earlier!" He hissed the words through his teeth as he glowered at John.

"I want some answers, Priest." He stepped closer. He pulled a picture out of his pocket and kneeled down in front of him. "This was my friend Charlie. You know, the one you killed outside of Sun Tree a few days ago. Remember? Now I wanna hear you say it."

Priest said nothing. His eyes turned murky and he stared at him, keeping tight-lipped.

"I'm going to kill you, Priest." He stood up, stuffing the picture back into his pocket. "I'm going to kill you right now. It doesn't matter if you admit it to me. Your life ends now. You never should've—"

Wham!

Something huge and heavy struck the back of John's head. In front of him, the whole world looked wavy and out of focus. A million stars swam in his vision; shocked, he didn't even feel himself drop to the ground. A few confusing seconds went by, and the stars cleared. His vision was still blurry, but he could make out two figures towering over him.

A man with a purple-spiked mohawk and no shirt was standing over him with a lead pipe in his hands. Standing next to the pale-faced man was Priest. He grinned from ear to ear, like a demented jack-o-lantern from a cartoon. He pulled something out of his jacket. It was a sleek-looking Mac-10. He pointed it at John's face.

"What's your name, dude?"

"John Cutter." He rubbed the back of his head, checking his palm for blood.

His grin turned into a shark-toothed smile. "Not anymore. Goodnight, John."

Click.

"Fuck!" Priest cursed himself for not re-loading his gun, and turned to the shirtless drug addict. "Kill this asshole and come outside. They need us."

The pale assassin nodded, and Priest dropped his Mac and ran out of the warehouse. The man with the heavy pipe stared after him for a minute, lost in some kind of coked-up bliss. He turned his focus back to John, smiled, then raised the pipe over his head.

John rolled away as the Punk swung downwards, hitting the concrete with the pipe. He hit him in the side of the neck with a karate chop, grabbed his pipe and clubbed him over the head with it. The man instantly went down without a fight. Standing over him he made sure he was out, then threw the pipe behind him.

He scooped up the gun Priest had dropped earlier, tucked it in the back of his pants and pulled his shirt down over it. Searching around he saw a clip to the Mac in an open crate. He grabbed it, slapped it into the gun, then tucked it back inside of his pants. He started towards the doorway; he swiftly paused and turned around.

The Mac-10 wasn't the only thing that Priest had dropped. Smiling, he reached down and grabbed the grenade, and shoved it in his other pocket. John took a deep breath, then prepared himself for anything as he stepped out into the raging streets.

TEN

IT WAS A COMPLETE NIGHTMARE OUTSIDE.
Gutter Street and Anarchy were tearing into each other like wild dogs. Bodies were being tossed through windows. People were being stabbed, shot, and beaten to bloody pulps right before his very eyes. There was no sign of Priest, though. The two rivaling clicks didn't seem to notice him as they clashed. Fine by him. The only person he wanted to shoot was the man responsible for Charlie's demise.

    Police sirens filled the night air. Out of nowhere, dozens of cop cars appeared. One of them plowed right into the fighting crowd, sending Punk and GSM member alike flying through the air. Two vans with the words BayView Police painted on the side of them rolled up, and the back doors swung open. Ten men dressed in riot gear piled out of the first van with M-16s in their hands. Ten more jumped out of the second, armed with night sticks and shields.

    Tear gas was generously thrown into the crowd. Gang members were beaten, maced, and cuffed. In all of the confusion, gangs from both sides took off running in different directions. John saw one of them escaping towards the KingStreet tunnels to the subway.

    Priest!

John took off after him, avoiding the cops. No way he was getting away. Michael Priest would pay with his life.

John chased Priest through the tunnels, the warm night air whipping past him. He pumped his arms and legs wildly, desperately trying to close in on his enemy. To the right of them a subway train roared by, making the ground shake. Still running at top speed Priest turned and grinned menacingly. He made it to the stairs and darted up them, skipping two and three at a time.

John ran up the stairs and made it to the top. Priest had vanished. He glanced around, frustrated, trying to think of where he could have gone. He ran through the slums of BayView until he reached KingStreet. He was back in the heart of Priest's territory now. He narrowed his eyes, mentally putting his defenses up.

He moved down the streets, ready for anyone that might leap out from an alley and bust him in his head. Two women in tight, short dresses stood under a flickering streetlight. He could see the red dots from the cigarettes in their hands. As he moved closer they seductively eyed him up and down.

"Hey baby, you want some company tonight?" The blonde one stepped forward. She reached out and grabbed him by the arm, pulling him towards her.

The other girl with black hair and a short, blue dress stepped behind him, whispering filthy things into his ear. John gently pushed them away and made his way down the street again, taking in his surroundings.

"Aw, he's a virgin," the black-haired girl said, poking her lips out. She made a mocking sad face as she teased him more. "What's the matta' baby, you scared of girls? Don't worry I'll pop ya' cherry for ya'!"

The blonde one chimed in, enjoying the game. "Yeah come on back virgin…you need some drivin' lessons? I can ride you all night long, baby boy! We'll have you climbing the walls!"

She cackled viciously, the laughter making John…scared. She was actually *scaring* him, shit they both were. He hated to admit it, but it was true. He ignored their taunting and moved on, turning his focus back to the streets.

A few minutes past by…and still no sign of King Punk. He glanced to his right and saw the shimmering water of the Bay. He walked over to a guard rail and stood for a second, awe-struck.

"So much violence and death around me," he said, whispering under his breath. "It sure is nice to see something…peaceful for a change."

The sound of the water calmed him, the waves soothing to his soul. He marveled at the view, enjoying the serenity.

"Gimme' your wallet, bitch!"

He turned around when he heard the gruff male voice. To the left of him was a dark alley with dumpsters and trash cans. A shadowy figure was standing over a woman.

"Help me!" she screamed, hitting the thug's arms. "Somebody please!"

"Shut up!" The man grabbed her by her neck and shoved her into the wall.

John sprinted across the street and hopped over a dumpster. He ran into the alley, catching a glimpse of the frightened girl.

"Let her go!" He reached out to grab the man.

Surprised, the thug spun around and shrank away from his reach. He pulled out a switchblade. "What do ya want, asshole?"

"You okay miss?" John asked her, scowling at the robber. He moved closer to the burly shit head and clenched his fists.

"I'm the one ya need to be worried about!"

"You know, I see you bothering this poor girl from across the street…and I ask myself why?"

The robber waved his switchblade. "Just get outta' my fuckin' face! Who are ya?"

He stood in front of the greasy, flat-faced hood and smiled. "Your worst nightmare."

The smelly robber took a swipe at him. John dodged it and kicked the man in the back, sending him into a pile of trash. The man pushed away from the garbage and jumped to his feet. He caught his breath and rushed towards him with his blade.

John grabbed a beer bottle and smashed it over the man's head. He dropped his switchblade and fell, cursing and screaming. He grabbed the man by his collar and dragged him to a dumpster.

"Let go of me, asshole! Let go!"

He ignored his pleas and banged his head against the dumpster. He picked him up and tossed him inside, then closed the lid.

He walked back to the dark-haired girl and helped her up. "Are you okay? Did he hurt you?"

"No." She brushed dirt off of her skirt and looked up at him. Her wide eyes were fearful. "He, he just scared me, that's all."

"What's your name?" he asked. He picked up her purse and gave it to her.

"Racquela," she stuttered. "…I w-was on my way home f-from work."

"Well you shouldn't be out here. It's dangerous." He glanced away from her and stared at the moon. "Do you live far?"

Racquela shook her head. "No I'm right around the corner. I know it's bad out here, but I still don't know why—"

He cut her off. "You should go home now. Here, take this with you."

He leaned down and grabbed the busted glass bottle. He handed it to her.

"Okay," she said, not sure what to say next.

They walked out of the alley and stood in the street. She started to say something to him, but hesitated. She turned and walked to the corner then paused again. She smiled and walked away. John watched her until she moved quickly down the street and disappeared around a corner. He sighed and went his own way.

After a few blocks he came to a place called the Pool Hall, the neon letters glowing white on the wooden building. A wino dressed in a brown trench coat sat against the place, holding his bottle of alcohol wrapped in a brown paper bag. The bearded man slurred something, then took a swig. John sighed, fighting the butterflies in his stomach.

He stepped off the sidewalk and moved across the street to the looming place in front of him. Two large windows showed people inside walking around green tables, shooting pool. Because the glass was so dirty he couldn't make out their faces, or how many there were. He pulled the smudged door open and stepped in, disregarding his fear.

The inside was just as shitty as the outside, just as he'd suspected. Punk Rock music blared through all of the speakers, the noise rattling his skull. The air was rank with cigarette smoke…and that familiar herbal scent he'd smelled on Gus earlier.

Punk chicks glared at him as he moved cautiously through the sea of drugged-out, wasted youth. A man with shades and a blue mohawk stood up from the pool table, mean-mugging him as he moved past.

"Excuse me," John said, at least trying to make an effort to be polite. The man made no indication whatsoever that he would move. John narrowed his body and moved past the heavily-tatted punk-rocker. He gripped his pool stick and lifted his shades with his other hand. He blew smoke in his face, then gave him a *come at me dog* look.

He ignored the disrespect, fighting the urge to bounce the man's head off the fucking walls. He caught more hateful stares as he made his way for the bar past the horde of rude patrons and pool tables.

Oh yeah, this was a great idea. I'm sure these folks would be more than happy to help me with any questions I may have. Ol' zombie lookin' muthafuckas...

By the time he'd made it to the bar his heart was thudding so hard in his chest it hurt him. In between two punk-rocker chicks was a lone bar stool. He went over to it, feeling awkward as he sat down. They glowered at him, regarding him hatefully.

He looked straight ahead at the bar shelves, ignoring them. *That still doesn't change the fact that they mean-muggin' the shit outta me right now* he thought. A hot ash from one girl's cigarette fell onto his forearm. He glanced down and brushed it away—

—and felt his blood freeze when he caught a glimpse of her hand. The letter *A* was tattooed on it. He casually glanced around, and noticed that the letter was everywhere, on the backs of jackets, shirts, tatted on arms and necks.

"Fuck me," he muttered darkly under his breath. He'd picked a fine time to come in the Pool Hall tonight.

"Can I help you?"

John flinched inwardly and looked at the huge, shirtless bar tender. He had a spiked mohawk and his arms were sleeved out with tattoos…and of course, the letter *A* was inked on his chest. He realized that the bar tender was asking him what he wanted to drink.

Great. Even the damn bar tender is in the gang. This must be Anarchy's watering hole.

John had never drank at a bar before. Sure he'd drank beers with his friends back home, he'd always been able to get alcohol because of their fake IDs, but this was different. He hadn't tried liquor yet. He tried to think of that dark drink that his dad used to always have.

"Jack n' Coke," he answered, trying to sound as cool as possible.

The bar tender scowled at him for a moment, then turned around and fixed his drink. He put his elbows on the table and leaned forward, praying the butterflies in his stomach would stop.

"You ain't from around here, huh?"

John's eyebrows raised. He looked at the girl to his right, shocked that she was speaking to him. "How you know where I'm from?"

"Cuz I can look at you and tell."

He stared at her a moment, trying to read into the question. The girl's pink hair wasn't spiked like the other thugs around him, it was a reverse mohawk. The sides of her head was shaved and she had a nose ring, the chain of the ring connecting to her ear. Her white tank-top had slits in it, exposing her large cleavage. Tattoos of dragons and skulls covered her arms and back.

"What the hell is that supposed to mean? You don't know me."

She smiled, her green eyes sizing him. She flicked more ashes from her cigarette. "Nah, you ain't from here. You're from the suburbs."

"Seven-fifty pal," the bar tender said. Somehow the way he said *pal* didn't sound to friendly.

"Uh-huh. And how you know all this?" John asked, offended by Pink Hair's comments. He reached inside his pocket and pulled out a ten, putting it on the bar.

Pink Hair's grin widened, exposing her white teeth. She snatched up the ten and gave it back to him. "It's okay Vince. Put it on my tab."

John was surprised the bar tender didn't even ask for his ID. He also didn't appreciate this chick paying for his drink, he didn't need anybody's charity. He took his drink. "You ain't answered my question. How you know all this?"

"From your nice-looking tennis shoes, to your clean-shaven face, to the way you drink your drink...you *scream* it."

"Yeah," he said, sipping his Jack, "right." Pink was beginning to irritate him. At least the Punks were ignoring him now, they had gone back to shooting pool and talking shit.

Pink looked over and smiled at the red-haired girl sitting next to John. She also had a reverse mohawk. Both women were grinning now, staring at him.

"So what are you doing over here, suburbanite?"

Before he could answer Pink he felt the peaceful atmosphere change. She stopped smiling and glanced behind her, obviously not happy about who'd just walked in. A couple of Anarchy members with bruised faces were talking wildly, agitated about something. She noted the one with purple hair. She leaned towards John, her warm shoulder touching his.

"I think you better get outta here," she whispered. She pulled a-hundred-dollar-bill out of her black jeans pocket and slid it towards Vince.

"Why?" He glanced down at his drink, noticing for the first time how dirty the glass was. He caught a glimpse of the red-haired girl getting off of her bar stool.

"Because some people around here don't like strangers. Especially suburbanites."

She took one last drag off her cigarette, then grinded it out in the ash tray. She grabbed his arm and stared at him gravely, her green eyes betraying nothing. He casually glanced up at the broken mirror over the bar, and saw two Punks. He tensed when he noticed the one with purple hair.

"Get out now." And with those final words Pink turned and headed for the door, leaving with Red.

John glanced into the mirror again and watched them leave the Pool Hall. The two Punks who had came in were glancing around, arguing. They stopped yelling when they saw

him sitting at the bar.
> *Ah, shit. This is not good.*

ELEVEN

"WELL LOOK WHO WE HAVE HERE!"
The Punk with the green mohawk said to the other man. They strolled over to the bar and sat down next to John. He recognized them from the gang fight earlier. His skin prickled as he fought with his nerves.

"Look who it is Psycho!" the man with the green hair yelled, slamming his hand on the bar. "It's our friend...Soul Brotha!"

"What are you doin' here, asshole?" Psycho said, not as amused as his friend was. John noticed a thick scar on his neck. It was the type of scar someone got from getting their throat slit. Whoever tried to kill him wasn't successful, unfortunately.

"Let's take this asshole outside Trash," Psycho hissed.

Trash smiled wide. "That's a good idea. Let's hit the road, Soul Brotha. Come on."

"But I haven't finished my drink," John said in a casual and antagonistic voice. He took a huge sip of his Jack and Coke, glancing down at the bar.

John wasn't a stranger to fighting. He'd seen more than his share of combat in the Army. He'd even had to kill for his country, so he sure as hell wasn't afraid to throw down. Being nervous was something totally different, especially when he was outnumbered in a pool hall full of enemies.

And now all my enemies are looking at me again. Damn they hella deep, too.

Every person in the bar was glaring at him, including people who weren't even in the gang. He quickly glanced at the two men on either side of him, then looked down at his drink. Trash was six-feet-four, broad shouldered, probably in his twenties. His face had a weird tint to it, like he was sickly. Skull heads and small dragons were inked all over his chest and back. The pale horse of death was on his right arm, a circled *A* on his left.

Psycho was brawny. The six-foot-two thug was ghostly pale, a three-inch scar on his left cheek. The word Anarchy was tatted across his stomach, the letter *A* on his back. His black jeans and boots were dirty from street fighting. Tracks covered the insides of his forearms.

"Well you're fuckin' done with it now," Psycho snarled.

Trash slapped John on the back. He grabbed his arm, his grip tight. "We're gonna' take a walk out back."

Trash nodded towards the rear door, an evil grin plastered on his sickly face. John knew if they took him for a walk, it would be the last walk he'd ever take. His body shook with adrenaline. A song he'd never heard before blared through the place's speakers:

"Schools are prisons!"

John closed his eyes and gulped the last of his drink, feeling the effects of the strong alcohol. He blinked them open and smashed his empty glass into Psycho's face. The surprised thug crashed to the floor, grabbing his face with his hands. He elbowed Trash in the neck, then grabbed his arm and flipped him over the bar. He crashed into the shelves of alcohol, the rows of bottles shattering as they hit the floor.

Crack!

Flashing stars of black swam in his vision. Someone had hit him with a cue stick. His focus cleared when he shook his head. He was on the floor, staring up at a mob of Punks stomping him. The asshole with the sunglasses was the one who'd cracked him in the head. He was hitting him now, as a matter of fact.

A heavy boot cracked into his right side, breaking his ribs. Fists and boots slammed into him all at once, knocking the wind out of him, bloodying his face. John kicked the man with the sunglasses in his knee, breaking it instantly. The man fell backwards, bumping into a few fighting thugs, knocking them back to the floor with him.

"Schools aaaaare, priiisooons!"

John saw his chance. He caught the combat boot of one creep and pushed him backwards, sending him flying through the air. He rolled away from stomping boots and jumped up quickly. The thugs didn't miss a beat. Within seconds they circled him, but he was ready for them this time.

Knuckles from everywhere smashed into his head, face, and body. John put his hands up and swung on them, knocking a few out, beating one to the floor. Then he beat two. Then three. He was fighting the entire Pool Hall now, throwing haymakers at the mob, catching a few himself.

Vince the bar tender leaped over the bar and rushed towards him with a bat. He took a mighty swing—

—and missed John as he ducked. He hit two thugs instead, knocking them into a table where three civilians were sitting. Frightened patrons who had nothing to do with the fracas took off like bats out of hell, running out of the place. He grabbed the bat from Vince and jammed it in his stomach, then knocked him in the head with it.

"Aaaaaaaaaa!" Vince hollered as he sailed through the air, slamming into one of the pool tables.

Home run asshole! John thought as he pummeled the oncoming horde of goons. They were everywhere, jumping off tables with pool cues, coming out of bathrooms with switchblades. He knocked them away like an ancient warrior battling for his life. Psycho woke up and knocked over a bar stool as he got to his feet. He blinked rapidly, wiping blood away from the gash on his forehead.

"Motherfucker!" Psycho roared, charging towards the mob.

He lunged at John and grabbed his waist. Psycho slammed him to the floor and pounded him viciously. The bat rolled away and hit Trash's foot. He picked it up and hurried over to them, shoving other Punks out the way.

"Keep that motherfucker there Psycho! Do you hear me? Beat his fucking brains in! Smash, smash, smash!"

John chopped Psycho in the throat with his hand. The vicious Punk grabbed his throat and fell backwards, struggling to breathe. Everyone in the Pool Hall charged towards him, trying to kill him.

The Mac-10!

He jumped up and reached behind him, grabbing the machine gun from his waistband. He let loose.

Tat-tat-tat-tat-tat-tat-tat-tat!

Everyone scattered as John fired into the ceiling, the lethal weapon jumping wildly in his hands. Punks dove for cover behind pool tables. Some of them ran to the bathrooms, ducking as they went. Through the chaos he saw one asshole with green hair running wildly.

"Traaash!"

He aimed at Trash and squeezed the trigger. The Punk leaped behind the bar and scrambled away from the bullets. He chased him, machine gun fire spraying the bar, shattering liquor bottles and splintering the shelves. The Punk jumped over the bar and crashed through the side window, hitting the street, escaping into the night.

Click, click, click.

John glanced down at the Mac-10, shocked that he'd managed to empty the whole thing. All around him Punks rose slowly, peeking from tables and overturned furniture.

"He's outta bullets!" One of them yelled. "Kill the motherfucker!"

John looked around frantically as they sprang up from their hiding places. Within seconds they armed themselves with broken chair legs and pool cues. He dropped the gun and quickly moved backwards, looking for an escape. He glanced towards the long, dark hallway behind him where the bathrooms were.

A door!

Way in the back stood a lone, black door. He reached inside his pocket and smiled when he felt the grenade. He pulled it out and held it above his head, the sight of it making them back the fuck up.

"Listen up assholes!" He inched back to the hallway as the Punks stood, their knives and sticks still in their hands. Happy that he had their attention, he continued.

"Tell that mufucka Priest that I wanna know who killed Charlie! And I'mma be back every *night* till I find out who! Now since I know he know sumthin' about it, you tell that cocksucka to meet me in the tunnels!"

With those final words John pulled the pin and dropped the grenade, then turned and sprinted down the hallway. As he ran to the door he heard the Punks behind him, shouting and running out of the building. He reached the door and yanked it open, diving outside as the hot night air engulfed him. Broken glass and dirt crunched under his feet as he ran towards a rusty dumpster thirty feet ahead. He pushed the top up and dove in.

KA-BOOM!

John laid inside of the reeking dumpster, struggling to catch his breath as the ground shook beneath him.

TWELVE

DANNY BOY'S NIGHT WAS FAR FROM over. Priest was on the rampage again, and tonight he had something special in mind. Something like robbing a liquor store, which was a favorite past-time of his. Once again Danny knew he was in for some shit when he was at Freddy's Fries. He was sitting at a bench outside eating a burger…when Priest came out of the shadows.

Priest staggered over to him with a bottle of JD in his hand. He could tell by the way he looked that he was on that powder again. He put his burger down and got up from the bench. It was time to get money.

"Danny Boy!" Priest shouted, his breath reeking of alcohol. "We're gonna have some fun tonight! We're gonna party on a suaray! You hear me? It's fun time. It's fucking fun tiiiiiiime!"

Danny wanted to tell him to slow down on that shit, but what could he do? This crazy man was paying the bills. He kept his mouth shut and did what he was told. Priest gulped the last of his JD and hurled the bottle into an oncoming car, shouting at the driver, daring him to come out of the Hatchback and do something.

He followed after Priest who kicked in the glass doors to the Mc Slushy's Liquor Store. They shattered, causing fragments to sprinkle the ground. He stepped over the broken glass and pulled out a sawed-off, firing it into the canned goods, blowing bottles of liquor to millions of pieces. He clutched the shotgun with both hands like a baseball bat, knocking over bottles of brandy and Wild Turkey, yelling at the top of his lungs.

Danny Boy stormed in and grabbed the clerk behind the counter. The clerk was broad-shouldered and about his size, and tried to take a swing at him. Danny dodged it and dropped him with a right hand, then grabbed the clerk's head and slammed it on the counter. There was visibly no more fight in him, the fear in the clerk's eyes charged him up, and he lost himself in the moment.

Two college kids the size of football players emerged from one of the aisles. They lunged at Danny, trying to bring justice to the store. He dove into the first one, pummeling him with combinations, punching his stomach, chest, and face. The other kid ran to his buddy's aid. He tackled Danny and tried to slam him.

Danny scowled at him. The ex-boxer turned around and hit the younger kid in the back with a few hammer fists. The third blow knocked him to the ground, and he started kicking and stomping the wailing kid. Satisfied, he turned to the first guy and beat him some more.

"Atta boy, Danny!" Priest cocked his head back and howled at the ceiling. "Fucking-A, you show em'! Look at you now, Danny Boy! Look at you now! Go, go, go!"

Priest spun around in circles like a loon, laughing, howling, screaming, lost to the point of no return. Shelves of bottles crashed to the floor when his arms made contact. Surveillance cameras were filming the entire crime of the two maniacs terrorizing the store.

Danny Boy stopped punching the bloody college guy on the floor. He turned around and realized that they were being filmed. He didn't like that. In a flash, he ran behind the counter and hopped over the unconscious clerk, then bent down. Just as he suspected, he found a wooden bat that was next to a black safe under the counter.

He turned the combination, knowing the code by heart, and opened up the safe. He grabbed a plastic bag and stuffed the money in, then stood and smashed the cash register with the bat.

Ca-ching!

Out the drawer flew, revealing hundreds, tens, and fives. He loaded up the bag until it bulged with cash. Priest was dancing his victory dance, holding the sawed-off above his head like a Tribal Warrior after battle.

Danny turned and swung the bat at the surveillance camera. He missed it, cursing the damn thing.

Outside blue and red lights flashed, the lights spilling into the store. Priest was oblivious to this and still dancing, spinning like a fucking idiot.

"Money! We got the money! Ah, ha, ha, ha!"

Danny hopped over the counter with the bag of cash. "Priest we gotta go. Priest we gotta go man, come on!"

He wasn't listening. He raised his gun and blew a hole in the ceiling. He was having the time of his life, unaware of the police.

"Priest the fuckin' cops is comin, yo." He tugged at his shoulder, trying to reason with him. "We gotta get out of here, man! Let's go!"

They ran out the store, looking in opposite directions. The police were barreling towards them. One of the cops was hanging out of the window with a service revolver in his hands, pointing it right at them while the other one was driving. Priest glared at them, then turned to his friend.

"Meet me at The spot Danny!"

Danny Boy threw the bag of stolen cash to Priest. They ran in opposite directions, fleeing from the cops.

John picked up the pace as he dashed to the Summerville Heights apartments, realizing that his injuries had once again healed. He could get used to this. He should've been dead a thousand times over, from his run-ins with the Punks, to King Eddie's slashing, and the massive ass-whipping he'd gotten at the Pool Hall. The radiation poisoning seemed to heal broken ribs as well, his breathing had returned to normal.

He moved to the back of the complex, not wanting the check-in girl to see him. He climbed the sturdy drain pipe to the second floor and grabbed the balcony to April's room. He opened her window and snuck inside, praying that she'd still be asleep.

No such luck. The peaceful darkness of the apartment disappeared as one of the light switches flickered on. She was standing in front of him. Her arms were crossed, a worried look plastered on her face.

Damn.

He closed his eyes and bowed his head. Definitely not in the mood to hear anything tonight, he'd been through enough.

"Where have you been?" Her voice was tight. "You just vanished without a word! And wha...what's all that blood on your shirt?"

"Look...I'm tired, alright? I just want to go to sleep right now. Found out a lot tonight but I'll tell you in the morning, okay? Right now I just wanna go to—"

"Oh, really?" She walked over and stood in front of him, blocking his way to the couch. "You learned a lot tonight, huh?"

John turned, trying to move around her. "Yeah."

"Well why don't you tell me about it now?" she countered, moving with him, blocking him again.

This was getting nowhere. He sighed and turned around, closing the window. He scratched his head and faced her, not sure where to start.

"I found out where Anarchy's hang-out spot is. It's this place called the Pool Hall, and..."

"What?" she yelled, interrupting him. Her tanned face burned red. "You went there tonight? Of course that's where they hang out, are you crazy?"

"I knew you'd act like this if I told you."

She put her hands on her hips. "Well how do you expect me to act? You could have been killed! No one goes there alone at night, not even the cops."

"Look," he said, moving close to her, "I just want to find out who killed my friend. Can't you understand that?"

"*No John!* Because you're going to get yourself killed in the process!"

He stared at her, his mouth agape. He tried to say something, but what could he say? There was no way to respond to that because she was right. He frowned and glanced away from her, staring at the vent in the floor.

April exhaled noisily and stepped to the side, letting him by. They both moved over to the couch and sat down, John moving to the other side away from her. She tugged at her blue shorts and crossed her arms again.

"Look I just don't want to see you get hurt, okay? I mean, I haven't forgotten how you saved my life. But that's no excuse for you to act so wreck-less. I'm sorry about Charlie, but there's a better way to handle this."

He didn't say anything. He stared at a painting of fruit on the wall instead.

"Just let the cops handle this, it's too dangerous."

He scoffed at that. "Yeah. What good will they do?"

"I don't know," she said, exasperated, "but they stand a better chance than a vigilante would."

"Yeah? Well what do you know? You ain't been in no combat. You never had to kill nobody to survive, so you don't know nuthin. Nobody understands."

She got up and sat close to him. They kept silent for a long time, the only sound in the apartment a ticking noise from a clock.

"Promise me you'll leave this to the cops…please?"

He didn't answer, his gaze fixed on the wall. He didn't want to hear it, his mind was made up. *She don't understand* he thought bitterly, *no one does.*

"Promise me John."

He stared into her soft, worried face. She was close enough to him that he could smell the clean, soapy scent of her skin.

"Okay," John said, lying to her. "I'll let the cops handle it."

Her face brightened, her sunshine smile beaming. She adjusted her white tank top, the shirt too tight around her chest. She reached out and touched his arm.

"So what happened out there? Your shirt—"

"Don't worry about it," he said, grabbing her wrist smoothly and rubbing her hand, "I'm fine. Just a little fight, that's all."

April stared at him, her face skeptical. "You don't look like it."

"Those…Punks. I started asking questions about Charlie and they beat me up. I got punched in the nose, that's why there's blood all over me."

"What?" She jumped up from the couch.

"They jumped me and threw me out of the place, so I came back here."

"Jesus John," she said, gasping. "You need to go to a hospital."

"Nah, I'm straight."

"I'll get you some ice."

He shook his head and waved his hand. "No, you don't have to do that. April I'm fine."

But it was no use. She was already in the kitchen. She pulled open a drawer and grabbed a plastic zip lock bag, then opened the freezer and filled it with ice cubes. He exhaled slowly as she closed the freezer door and walked in the living room, handing him the bag.

"Take this. No, don't lean your head back, just hold it on for a few minutes."

John put the cold-ass bag of ice on his nose. He chuckled to himself, remembering his childhood fights. The fact that he'd used to get socked out on the playground seemed hilarious now. A punch in the nose guaranteed a bloody one.

Yeah but if someone hit you in the nose now…

His smile faded. His body's ability to heal itself was bittersweet. The fact remained that he still felt like a freak, he wasn't used to it yet. He felt…weird.

"So where did you learn how to fight like that?" she asked, tugging at her shorts. "The Army?"

"Mell, mort ahb, moat ub," John tried to answer. He took the bag off of his nose and set it on the coffee table. "I mean, sort of. Most of it was from street fighting. I got picked on a lot when I was a kid, so I learned the hard way."

"Oh, wow." She covered her mouth. "I'm sorry."

He chuckled. "Don't be, it wasn't that bad. My dad put me in a boxing gym for a few years."

"Did you get any fights?" April asked, intrigued by his past.

"*Oh* yeah. I was twenty-and-sixteen, ten of them knock-outs. Won the Golden Gloves twice."

She got up and went to the kitchen. "Wow, that's good. It's too bad you didn't learn boxing earlier. Kids are mean."

He laughed again. "Yes. Yes they are."

"You look kind of young, though." She opened a cabinet and grabbed a coffee mug, honey, and a box of tea bags. She turned on the sink faucet and gestured the mug towards him. "When did you join the Army?"

"No thanks. I joined when I was sixteen."

"Bullshit." Her mouth dropped open. She filled the mug with hot water, put the Chamomile bag in, and turned the water off. She poured the honey in and grabbed a spoon, mixing it together. "You did *not*."

"Yeah," he said, chuckling, "it's true! I lied about my age. Did ten weeks of boot camp at FT Benning, then I got my orders."

She walked back in the living room, stirring her tea. "Is that where you met your friend?"

"No. I met Charlie in Brazil during the Falcon War."

She sat on the loveseat across from him. "Sounds like a lot to handle for a sixteen-year-old." She sipped her tea, staring at him inquisitively. "You and Charlie must've been close."

John smiled, nodding at his friend's memory. "Yup. Me and Charlie were very close. Knew him for two years."

John's smile melted when images of the jungle flashed into his mind.

"I saved his life the first night I was there. You see, we were fighting against the Falcon Army, a group of rebel Guerillas that took over that part of South America. They flooded Brazil with drugs and terrorism so we had to bring them down. During the war Charlie saved my life too, and I never forgot it. I can't tell you how many firefights we'd been through together. He was…"

John paused a moment, a lump rising in his throat. "He was my friend."

Painful images hit him like ocean waves. John remembered getting laid by Marianela, an older woman he'd met back in Denver. It was his last night there, the night he'd ran away from home, so she'd let him stay at her house before he'd left. Though they were never close he missed her, and had fond memories of her.

He thought about being in the bush with his combat buddies, playing the dozens and telling jokes before the enemy attacked. Seemed like every night he was there, they'd lose another soldier.

He thought about the atrocious things he'd seen in the

jungles, things that would swallow any normal person whole. Torture, murder, burning bodies…Falcon had done terrible things. Him and Charlie never would have made it out alive if they hadn't fought the way they did. Now he was gone.

"So…uh, what about your family? Are they back home?" April asked, changing the subject. She kicked herself inwardly for bringing Charlie up.

"Yeah," he said, the life returning to his eyes, "my mom and dad. They live in Denver."

"Oh yeah, that must be nice. I hear it's really beautiful there when it snows."

"It really sucks when it snows too," John said, "especially when you have to shovel it. Other than that it's cool, though."

April giggled at his play on words. John stared at her blankly. He didn't get it.

"Alright so enough about me, tell me something about you. You from here?"

"Nah-uh," April said. She held her mug with both hands, taking a sip before continuing. "I'm from San Diego. My dad was a Five-Star General in the Army, that's why I could tell you were a soldier."

She brushed a strand of hair from her face.

"Anyways, dad got tired of being away from us all the time. He retired when I was twelve and moved back to California to be with us. And we were happy because we missed him."

John nodded. "Wow, a Five-Star. He must call you all the time, huh?"

"Dad died of a heart attack," she said.

"I'm sorry to hear that. He must've been a good guy."

"Oh he was," she said, her eyes brightening. Her smile returned. "He'd spoil me and my brother rotten, he used to buy us toys and take us out all the time."

"I see," John said, grinning.

"So anyways I went to New York for four years, got a degree from Cazenovia. When I turned twenty-one I drove out here with my friend. We got jobs at Fabiano's, and I've been here ever since."

He looked at her, confused. "Where's your friend?"

"Christine? She moved back to San Diego, she got tired of the crime."

He nodded, still curious. "And you said you drove out here. Where's your car?"

"They stole it a month ago," she said, her voice bitter. "I'm pretty sure it was Priest and his goons, but I'll never know."

He glanced at the picture on the coffee table next to him and picked it up. April and an attractive young woman were in the photograph, standing next to a beige Hyundai Elantra.

"Is this it?"

She nodded. "That's the one. Loved that little car, too. Just paid it off—and then that happened. Of course, no one saw what happened. Probably wouldn't tell if they had, anyway."

"You know I never got a chance to ask you. What do you do?"

"I'm a Fashion Designer."

John stared at her, surprised. "For real?"

She pointed to the China Cabinet behind her filled with frames. "See that picture of the blue hat in there? I designed that."

"Damn," he said, shocked. "Is that why your place is so fly?"

She giggled. "That's right, I design clothes for a living. My passion is hats but I love making clothes, too. I also help put on fashion shows, sometimes in New York and L.A. when they want me to travel."

"That sounds like fun."

"Can I ask you something John? Why do you insist on wearing bloody shirts? I mean, do you want to change?"

He grinned, noting her sarcasm. She stood up, smiling at him.

"I dunno," he said, smiling back at her. "Can I ask *you* something? Who wears volleyball shorts at one-thirty-five in the morning?"

She stared at him for a second. "Shut up." She pulled at the tight shorts.

"Got a game tonight?"

"Oh shut up, John!" She scowled at him playfully, then picked up a pillow and threw it at him.

They both laughed, enjoying the exchange. It was welcoming for him, and for a moment he forgot about his troubles. She stopped laughing and stood still for a second.

"Shit!" she said, staring at the cable box clock on top of the TV.

"What's the matter?" he asked, genuinely concerned.

She ran to the sink and poured the rest of her tea out. "I can't believe how late it is, I have to be up in four hours!"

He watched her speed past him to her bedroom, and for the first time was actually happy about his situation. At eighteen he was already retired from the military, and getting checks on the first and fifteenth. With the amount of money he was getting he didn't even have to work at this point. And here she was rushing off to bed so she could get up early.

I certainly don't envy her.

April ran to the bathroom and came out with a fresh shirt. She threw it to him, then opened her door. "Listen I'm done for the night. If you get hungry there's plenty of food in the fridge. Don't know if you like pizza, but there's some leftover Chinelli's from the other night. Again, I'm sorry about the couch."

John smiled. "Nah, it's all good. The couch is actually—"

"Goodnight," she said, cutting him off. She slammed the door.

"—comfortable." John shrugged and laid down, his body sinking into the soft pillows.

Most people might have complained, but he was grateful for the couch. Two years of sleeping in trenches and on jungle floors made him appreciate the little things. His mind raced as he stared at the ceiling, thinking about the brawl at the Pool Hall. He wondered if the grenade he'd thrown had killed anyone.

It still amazed him that he was able to walk out of there alive. So many things could've gone wrong tonight despite the fact that he was damn near Superman.

Yeah right. Don't get too cocky John, you ain't no Superman. You don't even know if you have any other abilities, or why *this is happening to you. Maybe it's more than the radiation, maybe it's…*

John sighed. He closed his eyes and drifted off to sleep, too tired to think about it anymore.

THIRTEEN

"JOHN GET UP!"
He sat up and glanced around frantically, expecting to see a group of ninjas terrorizing the apartment. April was standing in front of the television with the remote in her hands. She threw the faulty remote down, cursing it for not working.

"Look what they're saying on the news."

She turned the volume up, then stepped back from the TV and sat on the couch next to him. He rubbed his face and leaned forward, focusing on the reporter.

"Good morning, this is Linda Chow reporting from Channel 4. I'm standing here in front of the abandoned C&C warehouse building in front of KingStreet. It seems as though terror has once again struck the city of BayView after a huge gang war erupted between the Anarchy crew and Gutter Street Mafia. After a brief scuffle police and S.W.A.T. arrived on the scene to break up the melee, making hundreds of arrest. A reported thirty-one Punks and twenty-five Gutter Street members were taken into custody, along with other suspected gang members. Among the arrested was the notorious Bricks, an enforcer for the Gutter Street faction. Michael Priest, who is the leader of Anarchy was believed to be involved in the violent scuffle, but is still at large. Police are currently looking for Priest and ask that anyone with any information on his whereabouts report it immediately to the BayView Police Department."

"And in unrelated news, violence at the local Pool Hall bar

frequented by Anarchy ended in an explosion after an unidentified man entered the place, and set off a grenade. Police have no suspects in this case, but arrested several Punks. So far they are not cooperating."

April's eyes lit up. She turned and nudged John's shoulder.

"Hey that's the place you went to last night! Why didn't you tell me about the grenade?"

John widened his eyes. "I didn't know anything about that," he said, pretending to be shocked.

"...John. John did you cause that explosion?"

"What? Hell nah, I didn't do that!" he said, lying.

He started to say something else, then stopped when he saw her face. She had that 'I don't believe you' look written all over her, an expression he knew all to well. His mother had given him that look when he used to sneak out at night with his friends.

"April, you gotta believe me! I ain't had nuthin to *do* with that! Look, after they beat my ass they threw me out, then I left and came right back here."

"You sure?" She uncrossed her arms and it looked like she was starting to buy it.

"Come on, huh? I may be wreck-less, but I'm not crazy!"

He laughed, and cursed himself inwardly for making it sound forced. Though his health had gotten better he had a lot of work to do on his lying. He tensely waited for her response.

"Okay," she said, sounding rueful, "I believe you. I don't know why I would even…"

John secretly rejoiced. He tuned her out, listening to the rest of the news.

"...your help in capturing the following suspect. His name is Daniel Porter, known on the streets as Danny Boy. Suspect is six-foot-three, approximately two-hundred pounds. He has black hair and green eyes, and was born in Brooklyn, New York. Mr. Porter has a tattoo of dark-green gloves on his left shoulder, and used to be a semi-professional boxer in his hometown. So far police have not been able to tie him with any BayView gangs or locate his whereabouts. Porter is believed to be a suspect in an unsolved murder case, and is considered to be extremely..."

John frowned, staring at her. "Where you going?"

"Sweetie, I have to go to work!" April raised her eyebrows and smirked. She got up and went to the kitchen stove, turning the boiling pot of tea off. "I mean *somebody's* gotta bring home the bacon around here."

"Yeah I can dig it."

"You want some?" She gestured towards the freshly made tea.

He shook his head no. "It's too bad these cops can't find the scumbags in this city and arrest them."

April nodded in agreement. Crime seemed to flourish here in the Bay and it didn't show any signs of stopping, especially with that asshole Priest and his goonies running around. They were the main cause of the city's problems. The drugs, the fighting, the shootings. Like everyone else she was getting tired of them running amok. It was time for someone to stop them. She couldn't deny it, she'd often fantasized about blowing them away herself.

She wasn't sure if she could do it, even with John on her side. Hell, she might get her brains painted on the sidewalk if she tried. She didn't have a snowballs chance in hell of stopping the gangs, but dammit, someone at least had to try.

"Jesus, I have to catch the six-forty-five bus to the subway. Then I have to get on the train and catch that to Fairfax so I can be at Fabiano's by eight."

She ran to the mirror on the wall, checking herself. Her silky, tannish skin was perfect, her lustrous hair slicked back.

Her black dress accentuated her curvy, athletic figure. The only thing off about her was the way she was moving, she was obviously not used to walking in high heels.

"Seems like every morning I'm in a rush," she said. "Damn I wish I had my car."

John frowned. He stood up and walked to her. "You're taking the subway? Shouldn't you have some heat?"

April smiled wryly. She pulled something out her purse. "I have this."

"A can of mace?" John took the mace and held it up like a smelly diaper. "Oh yeah, this'll do the trick! This ain't gonna do nuthin' against a *strap*."

"Well that's all I have John," she said, snatching it from him. "Look I may not be some…ring champion war hero, but I've lived here for a year. Okay? I know this city inside-out, so I can take care of myself. Got it?"

John signed, backing up a few steps. *Never took her for the sensitive type* he thought. He moved to the side as she huffed to the front door. April snatched it open and stood a moment, not looking back. He chuckled inwardly, then walked to her.

"Look I'm sorry, okay?" He squeezed her shoulder. "You're right; you've been in this city way before I came along. So who am I to tell you anything? I…look, just be careful, okay?"

April kept silent for a moment. She faced him, and he did everything in his power to keep from laughing when he saw her pursed lips.

"Um, I get off at four today, but I usually get back around five, depending on the buses."

"I'll be here," John said, grinning.

"Here's a spare key in case you decide to go out today. Now you don't have to sneak through the window anymore."

She gave him the key then walked out. She stood in the hallway for a moment, then looked at him. "You be careful, too."

    John watched April from the door as she hurried down the hallway and vanished down the stairs.

FOURTEEN

PRIEST AND DANNY BOY STROLLED INTO Karl's Credit to make their collections. Karl stood behind the desk, shaking. He mumbled a prayer as they sauntered over to him, shoving customer's out of the way.

"Yo dude!" Priest yelled. He drummed his fingers on the counter. "What do ya got for me today, Karl? Anything good?"

"Y-yeah Priest, sure," he answered, stuttering.

It was hard for Karl to earn a living with these two derelicts robbing him every time. And that's exactly what it was; robbery. He had to pay him for protection. Anyone who refused to pay Michael Priest was shark food, to him *and* the other gangs.

He reached for the manila envelope under the counter. Danny watched him viciously. He handed it to Priest with a shaky hand.

"Here you go man. It's all there, you can count it if you want."

"Hey come on now Karl, we believe you!" he said, pretending to sound hurt. "Don't we, Danny?"

The boxer didn't say a word. He stared at the store owner with dead eyes. Priest kept up his antics.

"What do you take us for, a couple of thugs? We're your friends. We always treated you fair, you know."

"Oh yes, of course you have!" Karl was trembling so bad he could barely move.

"We kept you safe when Guns tried to come around and shake ya down, right?"

"And I want to thank you for that, too. Everything's back to normal since you've kept Gutter Street out of here."

He stopped thumbing the money. He stared at him, his blue eyes cold. "And everything's gonna stay that way, too. Long as ya pay up."

He put the cash back in the envelope and stuffed it inside of his jacket. He glanced around the credit store…then stared out of the window.

"Mother *fucker*."

Danny got off the counter and followed Priest's gaze, wondering why he was suddenly so pissed. Kenny Crack was outside, about to walk into Karl's store. He saw them, cursed, and took off.

Priest and Danny bolted out of Karl's Credit and chased Kenny across the street, ducking cars as they went. Kenny somehow managed to keep his white fitted on. His gold jewelry flapped around, then snapped off his neck. He ignored it, clamoring into the Village Thrift Store, weaving around the shoppers.

"Where ya gonna go, Kenny?" Priest yelled. "Where ya gonna go!"

Frightened customers and cashiers gaped at the three goons running through the store. Kenny bolted down the isle of hand-me-down clothes and escaped out the back door, setting off the fire alarm. They both stopped in the middle of the isle.

"Go out front and around the side," Priest ordered him. "I'll meet you around back."

Danny Boy nodded. He turned and ran out the front door as Priest ran to the back, mumbling murderously.

Kenny stopped in mid-stride, glancing around like a frightened deer. The burning sun shone down on him, touching his face and bare arms with fiery fingers, bathing him in heat.

He panted and tried to catch his breath, angry with himself for wearing black jeans on such a boiling day.

When the coast was clear he sprinted towards three dumpsters. Out of nowhere a huge fist came flying into his stomach, knocking all the wind out of him. He laid on the street curled up into a ball, motionless. He struggled to look up only to catch a glimpse of Danny Boy's broad, ugly face staring down at him.

"You piece of shit," he snarled, his fists balled up.

Another giant, equally intimidating figure materialized next to Danny, the man's face twisted into a scowl. His mohawk seemed spikier than usual, the yellow-tips of the spikes dagger-like. He kicked Kenny in the ribs, not giving him a chance to catch his breath, stomping the rest of it out of him.

"Where's my fuckin' money Kenny?" He kicked him again.

Kenny Crack winced in pain from the kicks and punches. "I don't have it man! Yerrrgh! Just lemme' explain."

"You little fuck!" Priest exploded. He reached down and grabbed him by his collar. "Stand him up. Stand this motherfucker up now!"

Priest and Danny snatched him from the ground, each grabbing a fist-full of his white-t. He punched Kenny in the face, sending him flying into Danny.

"Where's my money?" he asked again, his voice hysterical.

"Priest please! I, I don't—"

"Where!"

Danny Boy back-handed Crack's face, leaving red marks all over him. He threw a hook to his body, sending him back to the leader of the Punks. They both took turns smacking him around in the alley.

"Guys, *please!* Gimme' a chance to explain, just don't hit me no more."

"Mufucka you owe us ten-thousand-dollars!" Danny boomed, giving him a fresh slap.

"You mean to tell me you spent all of that money?" Priest asked, his voice burning with anger.

"Nah he got somethin." The Brooklyn fugitive held him by his collar. "I know you do, son."

Priest stood next to him. "You skimming off the top?"

"No Priest, never. Please you gotta believe me…you gotta believe me! Yerrrgh!"

"You're stealing from me. I put you into action, you little cocksucker. I should kill you! I'm the one who let you move on the streets. Guns would've opened you up if not for me. I did all of this for you…and you fuck with me!"

As he drilled Kenny, Danny Boy reached into the dealer's pockets, taking his money.

"How much does he got on him Danny?"

The broad-shouldered thug counted Kenny's wad of cash, then reached in his other pocket, stealing his bag of rocks, too. He stared at the Punk leader, his expression unhappy. "Twenty-five-hundred, man."

Priest glanced away from them. He stared at the street a moment, nodding to himself. The man had long been stealing from Anarchy for *too* long.

"I was going to give that to you guys, I swear! Ah dude you gotta believe me. I, I, I was just holdin' that until I could get all of it! Please, man."

He scratched his mohawk, deep in thought. He looked at the dope dealer and made his decision.

"I'm gonna give you a break this time." He smiled at Kenny, exposing his shark-like teeth. He glanced at Danny and nodded.

"Oh God thank you," Kenny blubbered.

"Tell you what I'm gonna do," Priest said, shifting his gaze to the dealer again. He pulled his aluminum bat out of his pants. "I'll give you a choice, Kenny Crack. It's either your legs…or your balls!"

He tried to run but Danny Boy grabbed him, holding his arms behind his back.

"No Priest, don't!" He pleaded and tried to break from his underling's hold, but it was no use.

Priest moved closer. "Make a decision, Kenny. Make a *decision*."

Kenny Crack's face grew ashen as the criminals prepared to work him over. Two homeless men were by the dumpsters, one passed out, the other sipping on a forty-ounce, watching the scene unfold. Priest and Danny stared at each other.

"The legs," the two of them said in unison.

Priest wound up slowly, gripping the bat in his hands. He bent his knees and stood like a baseball player. He looked to his left…he looked to his right…he swung downwards with all his might, cracking Kenny's ankle.

The young dealer hollered to the top of his lungs. Danny let go of him, letting him drop to his knees. Priest showed no mercy and smashed his left knee. Then his leg.

"Auuuugh!"

Priest turned his back and glanced up at the sky, disgusted. "Ah shut up Kenny! I mean, give me a break, will ya? You brought this on yourself. You know that…don't you, Kenny? You gave me no choice."

He spun around and raised the bat over his head, running towards Kenny. He took a mighty swing and shattered his collar bone. He raised the bat again, standing over his other leg.

"You know what? I'm not gonna break your other leg." He lowered the bat, shaking his head at him. "Now hobble the fuck outta here and get me the rest of my money. Don't let me see you again, Kenny. Not 'til you have all of it."

"So what now? We going to hold up the liquor store again?"

He glanced at the boxer and shook his head. "No. Not now anyway, High's is too hot. Let's make a few more stops. Then we'll head to SkyLine."

Michael Priest and Danny Boy ran off to make more collections and left Kenny Crack behind, face down in the alley.

John locked the door and jogged down the stairs. He hit the streets and crossed Riverside Avenue, enjoying the BayView heat.

"With such nice weather who could stay inside on a day like this?" he asked himself.

Halfway across the street he heard two guttural growls behind him. He froze for a second, not wanting to see what he already knew what was behind him, not wanting to admit to himself what he knew was there. He turned slowly—

—and unfortunately, he was right. Two fully-grown Doberman Pinschers stood ten feet from him, growling, snarling, dripping ooze from their jaws.

I take it all back. Should've stayed my ass inside.

He turned around again and slowly moved forward. Maybe if he didn't show any fear and kept walking they'd leave him alone. His father told him a long time ago that if he'd ever gotten into a situation with a wild dog not to run. They wouldn't chase him if he didn't run.

"Woof, woof, woof!"

"Shit!" he yelled. He broke out into a full sprint.

The wild dogs barreled after him, chasing him across the dangerous street. Traffic whipped past him. Angry drivers screamed out of their windows, cursing him. As he sprinted he heard a car horn followed by a loud crunch, and a satisfying yelp. When he was all the way across the street he turned and saw one of the Dobermans' sprawled on the street, clawing the air.

The driver who'd hit the dumb dog sped away and

didn't bother to stop. Other cars ran over the animal at top speed, putting it out of its misery. The other Doberman changed its mind about chasing him. It turned and ran the other direction and disappeared behind the Summerville complex.

John turned and walked forward, searching for any more dogs. He honestly would've been fine if he'd fought with the dogs. They couldn't kill him, but there were too many people around. He didn't feel like showing his powers off to the whole world.

Low profile. That's the key, Johnny boy. Don't draw too much attention to yourself. The last thing you need is for some asshole to spot you, and run to the papers about it.

John looked up and realized that he'd entered the Riverside Apartments complex. This area seemed equally shitty as the rest of BayView. Dope fiends and prostitutes stared at him like he was some exotic creature they'd never seen before. As he got closer to the apartments he realized the dope heads weren't the only ones staring at him.

A group of young tuffs dressed in green were leaning against an iron fence. Some of them wore dark-gray bandanas on their heads while others had them tied around their faces. They looked at him sideways as he approached. He noted the one with sunglasses reach behind his back.

...can it be? A fresh, El-Camino Rollin Kilo—

An old-school rap song blasted out of a nice sound system, the sound of the music getting closer. A car rolled up behind him and drove by, the driver inside invisible, shielded by dark-tinted windows. It was a 1970 Cutlass Supreme SX with a white top. The Cutlass drove by him slowly and stopped in front of the tuffs.

John realized that as he neared them a feeling inside of him went off. His heart sped up, pumping adrenaline throughout his body. What he was feeling wasn't fear…it was excitement. It was the same type of rush he'd felt in the jungle.

I am not afraid. Do your worst.

Between him and the tuffs was a playground…an abandoned one, he noticed. He wondered where everybody was. Normally there would be kids on a freaking playground. The ground under him changed as his Air Forces left black asphalt and sank into playground sand.

Rat-tat-tat!

Gunshots came from everywhere, slamming into the swing sets and slides around him. He fell to the ground and ducked for cover as more shots went off. He glanced up, his hands still over his head, and realized that the bullets were coming from the apartment windows. Riverside had snipers.

The snipers kept shooting, their bullets smashing into the sand around his body. The tuffs he'd seen earlier had vanished. All the dope heads and prostitutes were gone, too. A loud shotgun blast filled the air, muffling the sounds of the automatic gunfire.

Glass shattered from a parked car as the shooting continued. John shut his eyes and wondered when the next bullet would blow his head off.

A lone figure appeared in the doorway to one of the main apartment buildings. The mysterious figure moved down the steps and started walking towards him.

Suddenly the gunfire stopped. As the person came closer John saw him more clearly. He was dressed in gray khakis and a matching gray shirt. Green bandanas covered his head and face. His All-Stars were green, matching his rags perfectly. Mystery Man moved closer, his stride unrushed.

John stood up and brushed himself off. Something about the approaching man intrigued him. When he'd walked out of the complex he was un-phased by the gunfire going off around him. He seemed unworried that one of the bullets could have hit him. Then the shooting just…stopped when he'd showed up.

Mystery Man stopped and stood in front of John. He was exactly six inches away from him, his reflection showing in Mystery's black shades. He blinked once. When he opened his eyes there were hundreds of young gangsters draped in green-and-gray, standing behind their leader.

"Fuck is you?" Mystery asked.

John kept his arms to his sides, mindful not to make any sudden moves. He sized the man up, noting the green bandanas wrapped around his smooth, dark skin. Every gangster behind him held weapons in their hands; pipes, sawed-offs, automatic pistols. They glared at him like a pack of hungry wolves after bloody meat.

"My name is John."

"Fuck you doin 'round here?" Mystery Man stood frozen, sizing him up behind his shades.

"What's your name?" he asked, not taking his eyes off him.

"Who are *you*? Don't you ever ask who this is!" one of the gangsters yelled from the crowd.

"Listen," John said, keeping still, "I mean you no disrespect. I also mean no disrespect to your neighborhood. A few days ago a friend of mine was killed, and I'm just trying to find out what happened."

No one uttered a word. It seemed as though nature itself had ceased to exist, the silence around them surreal. After a long pause Mystery Man nodded.

"Walk with me," he said, his voice muffled by the bandanas.

He turned and headed back towards the complex. John walked alongside him and past the sea of gangsters, feeling hundreds of criminal eyes following them. He noticed as they walked that none of his hoods followed him. They turned left off the main path and continued on a narrower sidewalk, leading to more run-down buildings.

"The name's Gary Washington," Mystery Man said, "but my friends call me Guns."

Well holy shit, as I live and breathe. I'm talking to the leader of Gutter Street Mafia himself. Wonder how many people have been shot down just for trying to get in here?

Guns stood at five-foot-eleven, and looked to be about one-hundred-and-sixty-five pounds. Though he wasn't the biggest person in the world his presence commanded fear. And respect.

"So what you doin' around here, man?" Guns asked without looking at him. "You *po*lice?"

"Nah I'm not the cops." John pulled his buddy's picture out of his pocket. "I'm trying to find out who killed my friend, that's all. He was gunned down at the Sun Tree Motel. I heard you were there."

Guns stopped walking and turned sharply to him. "What are you trying to say!"

Suddenly his whole demeanor changed. His swagger alone was enough to intimidate the shit out of the average cat, and he wasn't even *trying* to be. Now he was just downright scary. John sensed this immediately, observing his balled fists. Violence radiated off him in waves.

"I'm just saying what I heard," John said, his voice calm.

"Yeah mufucka I was there, but I ain't kill nobody," he said through gritted teeth.

They stood in silence, staring at each other. For some reason John believed him. He was one-hundred-percent positive that Guns had been responsible for tons of violence, including murder, but he didn't think he was the one who off'ed his friend. He would have sensed it, somehow.

And if he had been responsible, I'd kill him here and now. Even if his buddies shot me down.

"Alright," he said, nodding.

Guns relaxed. He un-clenched his fists. The

atmosphere around them seemed to change, it was less tense somehow.

"That's messed up what happened to your boy, but you're looking in the wrong place."

John's eyes widened. "What do you mean? Who should I ask about this?"

"Man ask them crazy-ass white boys!" He turned and swatted at the air, agitated.

"You mean the Punks? Anarchy?"

Guns nodded, crossing his arms. John could feel the hatred coming from him as he spoke about his enemies.

"Let me tell you something John. Michael Priest didn't used to run things here. BayView was ours before he came in and took over, he's the one causin' shit. When you turn on the news, what do you see? Who do you hear about ninety-nine percent of the time? It's him man, and don't think for a second if his numbers was down that I wouldn't take his shit, too."

"Yeah but—"

He cut him off. "Riverside is mine. That belongs to Gutter Street. KingStreet, 125th, Montbello…he can have all that, I don't *care*. But Riverside is mine. I won't let anyone take that from me."

John glanced up at a window and saw a shooter. His face was covered by a rag and he was staring through a scope, aiming a rifle at his chest. He slowly turned around in a circle, spotting other shooters in different buildings, all of them aiming high-powered rifles. He glanced back at Guns.

"So what can you tell me about—"

"Time to go now John," he said, interrupting him again.

John could tell by his tone that Q & A time was over. He was done talking, and it was time for him to be on his way. He had so many questions for him, though. Guns brushed past him, leading him away from the hot zone.

He sighed, following him to the Riverside welcoming

sign. He faced the leader of the infamous GSM. Guns made a fist and covered it with his other hand, resting them on his chest.

"I'm gonna give you a break this time, something I normally don't do. But next time you come around here unannounced, I'll kill you. When you hit Riverside Avenue you keep on walkin', got it? You don't move in the zone unless I give you a pass."

"Alright," John said, nodding.

Guns turned away from him and strolled back to the apartments, joining his band of thugs. And with that John took his cue and left, hurrying down the street, away from the complex.

John wasn't afraid of GSM. All the bullets in the world wouldn't have stopped him. He just didn't feel like getting shot today, especially in broad daylight. He'd just have to settle for the info Guns had given him.

John glanced up and saw the Freddy's Fries restaurant ahead. He'd wondered how long he'd been walking for, then decided he didn't care. He was hungry and tired. Right now getting something to eat sounded like a good idea, even if the food was shitty.

And I know for a fact it is, I can smell the grease from all the way out here. Ah, well.

A woman in tight blue jeans and a t-shirt was sitting on one of the outside benches, sipping her soda. She brushed her curly-blonde hair out of her face and glanced up at him. A strange feeling of deja-vu came over him as he stared at her round, blue eyes.

Where do I know her from?

He looked away and walked into the restaurant. The smell of oily food was heavy in the air, the aroma making him want to turn around and leave. There wasn't a person in the place, all the customers were at the drive-thru. Fries and sticky soda covered the black-and-white-tiled floor.

At the counter he came face-to-face with Jessica, a young-looking blonde. Her blue shirt and black pants were covered in grease, like the other two girls behind her. She stared at him, her gaze blank and unenthusiastic. She didn't even bother to greet him. He glanced at the menu above her, unimpressed with the selections.

John was thrown off by the mute cashier. "Um…yeah. So I'll have the Special Fries then."

Jessica's eyes brightened, her heart-shaped face coming to life. Suddenly the dull mood changed, and the other two girls glanced up. Even the girl at the drive-thru window was staring at him.

"Do you want extra salt?" Jessica asked, her voice guarded.

"Yeah, what the hell. Give me extra salt."

"Will that be all for you sir?" she asked, glancing around nervously.

What the hell is going on? John wondered as Jessica motioned him to move behind the counter. The other two girls nodded, indicating it was okay for him to do it.

"Would you follow me, please?"

He was getting anxious. He turned and moved behind the counter, confused. He glanced over at the girl at the drive-thru; she was taking hundred-dollar bills from the customers, giving them their food. Nothing unusual.

He followed Jessica and walked through the kitchen with her, then to the back. She opened a lone door and got behind him, ushering him outside. She closed it and glanced around once more, then reached inside of her pocket. She moved closer to him, her nose touching the side of his face.

"Here," she said, grabbing his wrist. She stuffed a plastic bag in his hand; the bag felt bumpy. "That's five."

John glanced down at the bag, realizing that she was trying to sell him crack.

"Wait a minute...what?"

She lowered her voice to a whisper. "Two-for-five. Come on mister, I have to get back inside."

"What?" He stared at what he was holding, stunned. "Are you really trying to sell to me?"

"Yeah, that's what you wanted! *Special* Fries? Extra salt?"

"Yeah," John said, raising his voice, "but that's what I wanted...some actual fucking fries!"

Now Jessica looked stunned. "But...I saw you coming from the apartments! Guns didn't send you here?"

"Man hell nah!" he answered, jumping back. "Are you crazy?"

"Oh my God." Jessica turned away from him. "Oh, God. Please don't tell Guns what I did, okay?"

John fell against the brick wall behind him, still holding the large rocks in his hand. He couldn't believe this woman actually tried to sell him crack-cocaine in the Freddy's Fries restaurant. Just when he'd thought the Bay couldn't get any more shadier. Jessica turned and faced him, her green eyes fearful.

"Please mister," she said, grabbing his wrists. "Please don't tell him! I didn't know you really wanted the fries. If he finds out I took you out here, he'll—"

"Hey you know what? Don't worry about it," he said, handing the bag back to her. "I did come from Riverside. I was talking to Gary...er, Guns earlier, yeah. But that was about something else."

The girl was visibly shaken. He suddenly felt sorry for her and wondered if she was still in school. He gently squeezed her shoulders.

"Tell you what. I won't say nothing if you won't, okay?" He stared at her and smiled, cocking his head to the side.

Jessica gave him a shaky nod. "Yeah...yeah, okay."

John let go of her and leaned against the wall again, still floored by what'd just happened. She stuffed the drugs back into her pocket as he stared at her in disbelief.

"So you mean to tell me that he's got everyone slangin' out the Freddy's Fries?"

She Shrugged. "Yeah. I know it's cruddy but we're just trying to live, you know? Gary keeps us safe from the other creeps around here. He even keeps his own crew away from here, they only show up to collect. The Spikers come here too, everybody has to kick up to Priest."

John looked confused. "Spikers?"

"Yeah Spikers. Another name for Punks around here. At least that's what Gary calls them."

He rubbed his chin. "Gary told me that the Punks might have something to do with Charlie's death. I dunno though, maybe one of his boys did it, and he's covering for him."

"What are you talking about?" she asked.

He took out the picture and handed it to her. "My friend was shot at Mr. Lang's place a few days ago. Gary told me himself he was there, but said GSM had nothing to do with it."

"That's right," she said. She handed it back to him. "Gary's crew didn't kill your friend."

John eyed her suspiciously. "How do you know?"

"Because I was there with him that night."

He squinted his eyes. He folded his arms and nodded, eagerly waiting for her to continue.

"Guns…well, I like to call him Gary, picked me up when my shift was over. He said he had to stop by Lang's first to make a pick-up. When we got there Gary and his friends got out of the car. To make a long story short they found out that Priest had already been there and took GSM's protection money. They started arguing, and Gary said he'd be back to get it."

John was getting more disgusted as Jessica told her story. As far as he was concerned all of these bastards were the same. GSM and the Punks were both scumbags that terrorized the innocent. They were parasites, living off of ordinary people using fear. He kept his opinion to himself as she spoke.

"Gary drove back to Riverside and dropped his boys off, then took me home. He stayed with me and my roommates the whole night. You have to believe me mister, he had nothing to do with this."

He rubbed his chin. "So if his crew is not responsible for this, then who is?"

"Who do you think?" she countered, her tone confrontational.

He could see the anger rising in her face, flashing in her green eyes. She put her hand on her hip. She was genuinely revolted by the mere mention of Priest's gang.

"I know that Gary's no saint, believe me I do…but he had nothing to do with what happened that night. There are three guys that you need to look at; Psycho, Trash, and Michael Priest."

John let the names roll over in his head. The more he thought about it, the more it made sense. Anarchy Punks were a bunch of cowboys out for power. Unlike Gutter Street they were looking to expand and take over, and were willing to go to war for turf.

"Are you going after Priest?"

John glanced away from the street and looked at her. "Don't worry about that."

Jessica's face softened. She shied away from his glance and stared at her black tennis shoes. "You know, I never wanted to get involved in this lifestyle. I'm just trying to save up enough so I can get away from all this."

He shrugged inwardly. "I'm not judging. You gotta do what you gotta do to survive."

He turned around and grabbed the door handle, then

paused for a moment.

"Let me just ask you something Jessica. What's the code name for cocaine here?"

"Ice cream," she answered, still looking down at her shoes. She stuffed her hands in her back pockets.

"Uh-huh. And X?"

"Cookies."

He nodded, impressed. "What about weed?"

She glanced up at him. "Caesar Salad."

John threw his head back and closed his eyes, laughing whole-heartedly. "Amazing. Come on, let's go back in before someone sees us."

He opened the door and let her go first. She turned around and looked into his eyes, her face covered with worry. "If you do go after Priest, be careful. That guy is nuts."

Jessica reached in her pocket and pulled out a switchblade. She grabbed his wrist and put it inside of his hand. He stared at her a moment, touched by her genuine concern. He smiled, giving it back to her.

"No you keep it. Besides, you need it more than I do."

He followed her as she hurried through the kitchen and made her way back to the front counter. John glanced over at the drive-thru, catching a glimpse of a glassy-eyed customer handing the girl a hundred-dollar-bill. He saw the girl put baggies of crack and colorful pills inside the paper bag, and hand it to the man.

"Fucking amazing," he whispered, grinning to himself as he moved from behind the counter.

He stopped grinning when he glanced out the window. The blonde woman he'd seen earlier was still sitting on the bench. Two shady-looking men dressed in dirty clothes approached. Within seconds they accosted her. The larger man with the buzz cut grabbed her arm, shaking her as his wiry friend snickered.

John bolted out the front doors. He rushed towards

them.

"Who's this asshole?" the wiry one said, his wife-beater shirt hanging off his bony frame.

John didn't say a word. He walked right up to the bigger man and punched him in the side of his head, knocking him out cold. He turned around and jumped in the air, hitting Wiry with a devastating spin-kick. The skinny man crashed into one of the benches, knocking the mustard over. Satisfied that neither creep was a threat anymore, he turned to the blonde woman.

"Miss are you—"

But she had already taken off. He watched her run all the way down Montbello street until she disappeared to the subway tunnels. John sighed and crossed the street.

"Looks like I have a train to catch."

FIFTEEN

JOHN MOVED THROUGH THE KINGSTREET TUNNELS without regard. He was too tired to keep on his guard, and at this point didn't give a shit if anyone jumped out to attack him. People with briefcases and cell phones crowded the tunnels, waiting to run on their mindless errands, waiting for the train to take them to their dead-end jobs. Two kids with fitted caps and Mp3 players stood by the benches, mean-mugging him as he waited for the train.

Little bastards should be in school he thought. He ignored them and closed his eyes, wishing he had a car.

"Hey asshole, where ya goin'?"

John opened his eyes, glancing around like the other shocked bystanders were doing. A man dressed in a three-piece suit hung up his cell phone and clutched his briefcase, pulling it closer to him.

"Yeah asshole, we're talkin' to you!"

He turned his head and glanced over to the source of the insults. Two men were running down the stairs, looking bloody and pissed off. It was the same two he'd knocked out at the fast-food place. The big man with the buzz-cut had a busted lip, his blood trickling down his dirty, white wife-beater. The left side of Wiry-Man's face was swollen. He had on brass knuckles.

John closed his eyes and sighed deeply. "Come on guys, gimme a break okay? It's too hot for this shit. I'm tired of all this."

"You hear that, Boo-Boo?" Wiry Man said to the huge guy. "He says he's tired."

"Fuck that shit," Boo-Boo said. His face was red as a

tomato. "Let's git em' Dirty."

Boo-Boo and Dirty crept towards him, obviously not content with just one beating for the day. The big man rushed him, taking a punch at him. He swung wildly, missing every swing. John ducked the last haymaker and pummeled him with body blows. The two teenagers with fitted caps were laughing and cheering behind him, filming the brawl.

"Yeah, that's what I'm talking about! Youtube, baby!" they shouted, egging the fight on.

John forgot about Boo-Boo's friend. He felt a hard blow to his back. Dirty had hit him from behind, trying to knock him out. He wound his fist back and swung wide. John ducked.

Dirty's blow landed squarely on Boo-Boo's chin, the punch knocking him out immediately. He fell to the ground with a mighty thud. Seconds later he was snoring. John landed two vicious upper-cuts to Dirty's chin, then hit him with an elbow smash. He picked him up and threw him into two newspaper machines.

"You guys stop it! I'm calling the police," a woman from the crowd threatened.

The sound of screeching brakes filled the tunnels, and he turned away from the sleeping thugs. The train had finally come. Without a word he boarded, wishing silently that no one else would bother him. He sat on the cold seats, the hard metal uncomfortable. The train jerked forward and sped off.

"Yo that fight was hell'a sick!" One of the annoying teenagers said. They were still filming him with their cell phones. "So what's your name, dog?"

"Subway fights!" the other one with the blue cap yelled. "You beat the breaks off of him. You wanna say a few words for the camera?"

John put his hand up to block the phone's lens. "Nah come on man, just chill."

The kids kept bothering him, filming and

commentating on their latest project. Damn, the last thing he needed was to have his face plastered all over the internet. He was trying to keep a low profile. He looked at the people on the crowded subway train, and realized that over half of them had seen the fight. He glanced down at his bloody hands, wondering if he was screwed either way.

"Why don't you guys just grow up?" A woman with brunette hair said. She was standing up, holding onto one of the railings. "Just leave him alone, it's obvious he doesn't want to be bothered."

"Mind your business lady," the one in the red cap said.

Her eyes widened. "Hold on, who in the hell do you think *you're* talking to? Don't you ever disrespect me, I will slap the shit out of you right now! Watch your mouth because I am not the one, little boy."

"Oh, shit!" His idiot friend started laughing, happy with the extra conflict. "You gonna let her talk to you like that, dog?"

John sat in silence as the brunette cursed the two teenagers out. He stared at the red spot on one of his shoes, and realized that it was dried blood. He wondered if he was going to have to kick anyone else's ass today—or the next day, or the day after that. He put his hands over his ears and tried to tune out the noisy passengers around him.

The train finally stopped. He jumped up as the doors hissed open and he bolted through, desperate to escape the racket behind him. He ran through the cluttered tunnels, weaving around the busy-bodies. Ahead of him to the left was a bathroom. He moved past the rude business men, bumping into them to get by.

"Fucking finally," he muttered under his breath.

The bathroom was filthy, the flickering lights above highlighting the graffiti-painted mess. Urinals were stained with yellow. Clearly they hadn't been cleaned in some time. The cream-colored tile was littered with papers and crack pipes. He rushed to one of the sinks and turned the water on, washing thug blood off of his hands.

John rubbed the cold water on his face and through his wavy hair. Closing his eyes he leaned on the sink, letting his mind drift. The sound of running water calmed him, and at this point not even the shit-soapy smell of the bathroom bothered him.

Crunch! Crunch!

Sounds of breaking glass shattered his peaceful moment. Behind him heavy footsteps echoed throughout the grungy bathroom. A second set of footsteps joined the heavy ones. The two people behind him stopped moving. He turned the water off, not bothering to look up.

"That's him," a soft voice broke the silence. "That's the guy who did it."

John sighed gently. As he leaned on the sink he wondered how much more fighting he would have left just to find justice.

The road to vengeance is a violent one.

Heavy footsteps moved towards him and stopped at the sink next to him. Whoever the person was they were huge. Squeaky faucet handles turned, and the sound of splashing water filled his ears.

"I seem to run into you in the strangest places," a gruff male voice said to him.

John opened his eyes and glanced up at the man—

—and was relieved to see Gus staring at him.

Gus rinsed his hands and nodded, saying nothing more. He was glad to see the biker, he thought for sure it was those two goons he'd been beating up all day. He turned the faucet off and shook the water from his hands.

"You been to Freddy's Fries lately?"

John stood up, puzzled by the question. "Yeah. How did you know that?"

"I believe you've met Birdy." He nodded towards the

young woman behind them.

He turned around, and to his surprise, saw the blonde he'd saved from Boo-Boo and his goonie friend. She stared at him, her round-blue eyes focused. He studied her oval-shaped face for a second, and a light went off in his head.

"Torchy's!" John said, excited. "That's where I know you from, I knew I've seen you from somewhere."

Birdy smiled for the first time. Her skin was slightly pale, but didn't detract from her beauty. She was stout and intoxicatingly attractive. This guy had great taste in women. Gus stepped in front of him. He was not smiling.

"You saved my old lady, John. I owe you one. That's why I'm going to do something for you."

John scratched his head. "I don't understand."

He leaned in closer to him. "The word has come down...Priest put a hit out on you. There's a contract on your life."

He stepped back, frowning. "Are you sure?"

"Look," Gus said, his burly arms crossed, "I don't stick my neck out for no one, and I stay out of beefs that ain't mine. You? I'll make an exception."

Birdy jingled her keys as he spoke. She hadn't taken her eyes off him since they'd entered the bathroom.

"Follow me," the biker said.

Without another word he turned around, exposing his patch to John. There was a large, green-and-blue leaf on the back of his blue-jean jacket. The words PEACE RIDERS decorated the top rocker, the letters an aqua blue. BAYVIEW was painted on the bottom rocker.

John followed them out of the bathroom. He was surprised to find that the tunnels were deserted as they moved through them.

"Hey," he spoke up, "this is going back to Montbello. I'm headed to KingStreet."

"Don't go to KingStreet until midnight," he said

without turning around. He moved quickly, ignoring John's concern.

One of the trains screeched to a stop and the three of them hopped on. They rode the empty train in silence, John feeling uneasy as they stared at him. He caught a glimpse of Gus's jacket. The front of it was covered with patches, a few of them colored wings. One of the wings was black with a skull on it, and he was pretty sure he'd earned it for murdering someone.

He didn't know much about bikers. He'd heard his father talk about them briefly back home. What he did know is that they were no one to fuck with, he'd read the papers about biker wars in different states.

The train stopped and he followed them off, silently protesting the fact that they were moving away from KingStreet. He needed to go after Priest, he felt that each second he wasn't pursuing him was a second too long. They ran up the graffiti painted, trash-covered steps, exiting the tunnels. When they reached the top John saw two colossal bikers, sitting in a Burgundy Monte Carlo.

"We're going for a ride now," Gus said, taking his jacket off as Birdy popped the trunk. She left the car and walked around to him, taking his jacket.

Birdy carefully folded his colors and put them in the trunk. She turned around and held something white in her hands.

"Sorry my man, but we have to put this on you."

"Gus what's this all about?" John asked.

Birdy stood in front of John. He glanced down and saw the blindfold she was holding.

"Look," Gus said, sounding impatient, "I can help you, but this is the only way. I can't have you knowing where our *hideout* is. It's two-twenty-one now, and we have a long ride ahead of us. What's say we get a move-on, eh?"

Birdy wrapped the blindfold around his eyes before he

could utter a word of protest. He saw the world disappear and heard one of the bikers get out of the car as she moved him back.

"Put him in the trunk," Gus said. "You're not going to be comfortable, but don't worry. You'll get used to it."

He felt himself being lifted up by the bikers. They placed him inside and slammed the trunk down. He heard them hop in the car and slam the doors. Seconds later the ignition was started.

John laid inside of the trunk, wondering if he'd just made a grave mistake.

Hours that seemed like days crawled by as he laid in the trunk of the speeding car. Gasoline and oily rags flooded his nostrils. To his surprise the smell didn't seem to bother him, the only thing killing him was the time. He still wasn't happy with them for putting him back here, but since Gus was helping him he didn't have much of a choice.

John was glad that they at least hadn't tied him up. If he wanted to escape all he had to do was kick open the trunk and hop out. He'd have some serious road rash, but oh fucking well. The option of fleeing was always nice. Loud rock music blared from within the Monte Carlo, the sound of it vibrating throughout the vehicle.

On second thought, being in the trunk isn't so bad. Their choice of music is terrible.

As time inched by he found himself straining to hear the songs from the darkness. They were listening to 70's rock music. Though he'd never listened to that genre he did recognize some of the songs. At least staying awake wasn't hard, it felt like he was at a live concert.

The only thing that bothered him was Birdy's driving, every time she swerved or turned too sharp, he'd bang around in the back. He wondered if she realized this—he wondered if she cared. Probably not.

"Hey motherfucker! Learn how to drive!"

The sound of Gus's angry voice was unmistakable. Someone up front had a serious case of road rage.

"I'll come out there and kick your ass! You...turn the car around, Birdy. No, turn the motherfucker around! *Turn it around!*"

John laughed to himself, enjoying the invisible entertainment. From what he could hear Birdy and the other bikers were talking...reasoning with Gus to stay in the car. They'd obviously hit some traffic, and good ol' Gus was losing his temper.

"No fuck you, Joag! I'm gonna kick this guy's—"

A loud truck horn drowned out the rest of Gus's ranting. After a few minutes the Monte Carlo rolled forward, then picked up speed and zoomed off again.

He laid in the darkness and thought about April. He wondered what she was doing right now, how her day was going, and if it was as exciting as his. Somehow he doubted it, she probably wasn't locked up in some car riding around with outlaw bikers.

A million other thoughts rushed into his head, and he suddenly felt exhausted. His eyelids were growing heavy. He found himself nodding on and off, fighting sleep. Whenever Birdy hit a bump in the road or made a sudden stop he'd wake up again.

He felt the car slow down and take a long, winding turn. When a full minute went by it came to a complete stop. Silence. Another minute went by. He didn't hear a peep up front, and wondered if someone was about to get their brains blown out. He felt like he was in one of those old mob movies where the boss found out who the rat was, and decided to take him for a ride.

Car doors opened and slammed shut. The beautiful sound of the trunk popping made his blood rush. He felt hands grab his arms and legs as he was being pulled out of the trunk.

The two men stood on either side of him. They grabbed his arms and forced him to walk, leading him forward to the unknown.

"Relax kid," he heard Gus say, "it won't be long now."

John could feel his feet sinking with each step, and realized he was walking on sand. He didn't hear any cars or noises that were usually heard in the city, and tried to figure out where he was.

They stopped walking and let go of him. Suddenly a pair of soft, feminine hands grabbed his arm.

"Wait here," he heard Gus say, his voice curt.

He heard someone knocking on a door. He cocked his head to the side when he heard it open.

"Ah, Gus. Right on time. Come in, come in."

John felt himself being pulled into a room. The door closed softly behind him as he was led to a couple of steps. The person leading him stopped him, then grabbed his head and unwrapped the blindfold.

Bright light stung his eyes. He caught blurry glimpses of Birdy standing in front of him. He closed his eyes. He blinked them open again, getting them used to the blinding light. He turned his head and looked out of the room's window. The two huge bikers that rode with them were standing guard outside.

I'm in the desert. They've taken me to some strange motel in the desert.

John caught a glimpse of a few cactus and rolling tumbleweeds before Gus moved over to the window. He closed the curtains. He pulled something brown and thin out of his pocket and stuck it in his mouth. As he lit it up Birdy sat down in one of the stained chairs.

Ceiling lights buzzed above them, brightening the cruddy motel room they were in. Huge stains the size of oil slicks covered the blue carpet. The walls around them were cracked and covered in filth. A smudged mirror on the wooden dresser showed a man standing behind John.

"Blink, meet my friend John," Gus said, taking a drag off the strange, brown stick.

"Hello sir. How are you?" The man stepped forward, extending his hand.

"What's up." John reached out and shook his clammy hand. He let go of it, wiping the sweat on his jeans.

He looked at the weird-looking guy and realized why his friends called him Blink. His blood-shot eyes opened and shut rapidly, as if he had something stuck in them. He was dressed in a nice-looking suit, his red tie matching his handkerchief and cufflinks. His skin was abnormally pale, almost to the point of looking sickly.

There was something about this man that John didn't like. True, he was a snappy dresser, but that still didn't change the fact that he gave him the creeps. Blink had this aura about him that seemed—

—*unholy. That's the word I'm looking for. This muthafucka reminds me of Count Dracula, all he's missing is the cape.*

"I need a favor, Blink. My friend here needs your help." Gus blew smoke into the air, filling the room with that familiar, rotten herb smell. He moved over to Birdy, handing her his mellow stick.

"Ah, of course!" Blink slicked his long, greasy hair back with his hands. He brushed past John and jogged to the closet.

The creepy man opened the closet door and pulled out two huge, black suitcases. He dragged them over and flung them on the uncomfortable-looking bed. He opened one, revealing an arsenal unlike John had ever seen.

Being in the Army John had been exposed to all types of weapons, but he'd never seen a Street-Sweeper before. Blink pulled out a large backpack from the suitcase, exposing more guns.

"So what do you need, my friend? A twelve-gauge? How about a nice Remington? Or maybe you fancy this MP5 PT? It's a true rarity, and a personal favorite of mine."

John scratched his head, not sure where to start. "Nah, I'm going to be doing a lot of running around. I need something light."

Blink's shoulders sagged. He put the MP5 back. His face brightened as he reached back inside the suitcase. He pulled out two guns.

"What about a 9-mm? Or maybe this Saturday Night Special?"

John took the weapons and held them in each hand. He closed his eye, aiming them at the door. He glanced over to Gus.

"I'd go with the 9," Gus said, nodding.

John gave him the Saturday Night Special back and put the handgun to one side. He glanced at the other assortment of weapons, feeling like a kid in a candy store.

"What's that one right there?"

Blink followed his gaze and smiled. He picked up the impressive gun and held it up. "Ah, good eye! This, my friend, is a 44 Magnum. It holds six rounds and has amazing stopping power. You like it?"

"I mean it's kind of big, but yeah. What the hell, I'll take it. Let me get that .380, too."

"Ah," Blink said, reaching for the gun, "the Snub Nose. Excellent choice. Let me get you some rounds."

Blink unzipped the other suitcase and opened it up, revealing tons of boxed ammo and shotgun shells. The look on his pale face was priceless, he really did enjoy his work. He was grinning from ear to ear, whistling as he rummaged through the ammunition.

"Would you like something else with a little more kick? Grenades, TNT, C4?"

"Uh, let me get some grenades. Matter fact, do you

have dynamite?"

Blink beamed with pride. "But of course!"

"Swag. Let me get that, too."

He pulled out two sticks of dynamite then stopped. He stared at John, and his expression turned serious. "I like you. You know what? I'm going to throw this bag in for free. It's about the size of two book bags. It's light, easy to carry, and has an extra zipper on the side and back."

He grinned again. He turned and went back to work, grabbing boxes of ammo and dynamite. He stuffed them inside the bag and zipped it up.

"How much do I owe you?"

He grinned and straightened his collared shirt. "Five-thousand."

John pulled out a thick wad of cash. He took three one-thousand-dollar-bills and folded them up, then counted out the rest in hundreds. He paused for a minute, then took an extra amount of cash and handed Blink six-thousand dollars.

"Thank you, sir!" He greedily took the money and stuffed it in an envelope, then placed it in one of the suitcases. "I hope to see you again, John. It was a real pleasure!"

"…Yeah, man. Likewise."

Gus pulled out a plastic sandwich bag full of dark-brown powder. He walked over to Blink and handed it to him. He turned to the bed and scooped up John's bag of weapons.

"Alright brother, you know the deal."

Birdy blew the rotten smoke out of her mouth and grinded the brown thing out into an ash tray. She got up and stumbled over to John.

"Ah Gus, come on! Is that really necessary?"

"You know the rules John. Come on now, it's six-forty-five, and we need to get a move-on."

John sighed as Birdy blindfolded him. As the door opened he mentally prepared himself for the long ride in the trunk.

SIXTEEN

"WATCH YOUR ASS,"
Gus said to John. Birdy finished unwrapping the blindfold. The giant bikers hopped back inside the Monte Carlo without a word, settling into the backseats.

"If you ever need anything, let me know." Gus pulled the heavy black bag out of the trunk.

"Thanks," John said, taking it. He strapped it to his back. "I will."

"Come by the club sometime, rookie. We'll have a beer and I'll introduce you around."

"Yeah Gus. I think I'll have to take you up on that. By the way, what time is it?"

Gus stared at him, grinning his outlaw grin. "Time for you to get a watch. It's eleven-fifteen, kid. Get your ass off the street and go home. It gets wild around here at night. But then again you already know that, don't you?"

Gus grinned wider and punched John in the arm. He brushed past him and hopped in the car, slamming the door shut. Birdy stuffed the white blindfold in her pocket and moved towards the Carlo. She paused, then walked back to John.

"Thanks," she said. "I owe you one."

She reached out and squeezed his hand. Before he could say anything she turned away and hurried towards the car. She hopped in and slammed the door. John watched the Carlo speed off and vanish into the night.

"Looks like I better vanish too," he muttered under his breath.

He ran through the dark streets of BayView City, the full moon above him casting faint shadows on the side walk. Warm air hit his face and arms as he rushed down Montbello.

Damn. This city has the uncanny ability of making me nervous.

He mutely rejoiced when he saw Summerville Heights, the dark-orange complex seeming more and more like home to him. He dashed upstairs, cursing the empty beer can that crunched under his foot. Satisfied that the coast was clear he unlocked the door and ran in the apartment.

"April it's me!"

John flicked the light on by the door. He tip-toed his way to the bathroom, praying that she wouldn't come out and see the big-ass survival bag strapped to his back.

"So how was your day? Don't mind me, uh, I'm just going to the bathroom!"

He shoved the hefty bag in the cabinet under the sink and quietly shut the door. For some reason the apartment was deafly quiet. He stepped out into the hall, perking his head up.

Maybe she's asleep. Fine by me.

Rubbing his chin he glanced around, still impressed at how tidy she kept it. There literally wasn't a speck of dirt anywhere, even the bookcase and tables were free of dust. Feeling good, he turned and started for the door—

—until something on the kitchen counter caught his eye. A blinking red dot was flashing on her phone. Curious, he moved over to it. He pressed the button on the black phone and glanced around again, suddenly feeling uneasy.

"Hey John, it's me. Listen I'm going to stop by the Sun Tree after work and check on Mr. Lang. I'll be home late tonight. If you get there before me don't wait up! Bye!"

Beep!

He stood still, feeling numb. The fact that she would be

foolish enough to walk around KingStreet armed with just a can of mace was mind-blowing to him.

And at night, too? What was she thinking?

His good feeling quickly turned to anger. He stormed out of the apartment and slammed the door, locking it. He checked the doorknob two more times to make sure it was secure, then turned and bolted down the stairs, praying that he would be able to find her before she left the Sun Tree.

April and Lang sat by the window in the motel, sipping their Green Tea and talking. An argument between two tuffs ensued outside. As they spoke of old times the argument erupted into violence. The tuffs started fighting, slamming each other onto the ground. April watched in horror as they grappled in the street, then disappeared out of sight, shouting and brawling.

"Mr. Lang you have to get out of here, it's too dangerous! You saw what happened the other day."

He stared at her, incredulous. "And go where? Who's going to run this place when I'm gone? I have no other place to stay."

"You can stay with me," she said, her voice pleading. "If it's money you're worried about I can help you. Plus I know Priest is leaning on you. If you don't pay him it's only going to get worse, so you might as well stay with me."

"No!" he thundered. He stood to his feet, startling her. "No son-of-a-bitch going to run me off!"

He banged the table with his fist, making the tea cups rattle. She sighed, frustrated that he was being so damned stubborn. He was too proud for his own good, something that had gotten him into trouble in the past.

April jumped at the crackling sound of gunfire outside, the staccato noise making her heart jump into her throat. She spilled some of her tea on her lap, unable to control her shaking hands. Seconds later shotgun blasts boomed, the blasts deafening to her hears. Screeching tires was the next sound—then, silence. The gunfight was over and peace had returned. She glared up at Lang.

"You see that's what I'm talking about! Why would you want to stay here?"

"I-I'm not scared. I will not let Punks scare me away." Mr. Lang steadied his shaking hand and picked up his tea. "I've been here for twenty years. This is my home, April."

She didn't back off. "You are so damn stubborn, you know that?"

"I'll be okay, don't worry." He glanced out the window and sipped his tea.

She frowned. "Ugh, you make me sick."

Lang laughed heartily, trying not to spit out his tea. He reached out and touched her shoulder, enjoying her irritation. She was not amused. She glanced out the window, her irritation suddenly boiling over.

"Where the hell are the cops?"

He wiped the tears from his eyes, trying to stifle his laughter. "Bah! You know well as I do they don't come around here. They never come, they don't care!"

April had only known him for a year, but she knew the more excited Lang got, the more pronounced his accent became. She remembered the first day she'd met him. She'd gotten lost trying to find her way around the city so she wound up at his motel. He'd given her directions to the BayView Tunnels and even let her keep a map of the city. They'd struck up a conversation afterwards, and had become great friends. Of course there was no way in hell she'd stay at the Sun Tree, it was too run down and unsafe, so she'd moved to Summerville instead. She'd still managed to keep in touch with him, making sure to check in on him.

"I wonder how John is doing," April muttered under her breath. She sipped the last of her tea and stared out the window, hoping that he wasn't being too wreck-less.

John crept down KingStreet, blending in with the darkness. He glanced up at a lone brick building to his right, spotting a white clock. *Twelve o' clock on the dot* he thought to himself, angry that the ride with Gus had taken so long. He moved past Marco's Bar, a burned-down building to his right. Staring at the old wreckage he couldn't help but wonder that maybe the Punks had something to do with the bar's demise.

He moved further—and froze in his tracks when he saw a hand-full of Punks appear around the corner. They were armed with bats…and coming his way.

Shit!

He shrank back to the alley behind him and ducked behind a brick wall, hiding in the shadows. His heart nearly jumped out of his chest as he waited behind the wall, wondering if they had seen them. Lewd jokes and loud, gruff voices were the only things he heard. They walked right past him and disappeared down the street, their laughter still within earshot.

John waited a full minute before he peered around the corner. Exactly one-hundred feet ahead of him stood the Pool Hall. The front door was damaged by the grenade blast, but there were still people going in and out—mainly Spikers, he noted. He cursed himself for not remembering where he was, this was not the place to take a careless stroll in.

He counted fifty of the thugs in front of the damaged entrance, armed with bats, kicking up dust and smoking cigarettes. They appeared to be guarding the area and looking for someone.

Yeah…probably me.

He had to cross the street, there was no other way around it. He closed his eyes and took a deep breath, then sprang from behind the brick wall. He sprinted across the street towards the Good Times Cineplex. A few seconds later he made it to the building, amazed that they hadn't seen him…and that this building had been burned down, too.

He sighed heavily, his heart rate still jacked from the close encounter. He got himself together and moved away from the charred brick wall. Too many mistakes could mean an ass-whipping, so he made a mental note to be more mindful of his surroundings.

He walked down a place he hadn't seen before since he'd gotten to the city. In front of him was a sign that said C Street. Judging from the graffiti this place also belonged to Anarchy. Circled *A* letters were spray-painted all over the walls, trash cans, and abandoned buildings. Broken beer bottles were everywhere, the sharp glass littering the streets and sidewalks.

Every few seconds a car would speed down the quiet streets. A feint glow from a red, neon sign caught his attention. As he moved down C Street he saw the word LEGZ flashing on a red building. To the left of LEGZ was the KingStreet Bank and Fun Times Arcade, both of which were closed.

Three more buildings stood to the right of the flashing one. He ignored them and ran to the only place that seemed to still be open. A closer look revealed that there was no front entrance, so he walked around to the left of the building.

A man seven-feet-tall with black sunglasses stood in front of a door. His presence was intimidating, his black clothes and shaved head adding to it. He glanced down at John.

"Where's your ID?"

John flinched back, startled by his question. He realized that he had stumbled upon a strip club, and this overgrown ape was a bouncer. It also occurred to him that he probably looked twelve-years-old. People were always shocked to find out that he was eighteen.

The bouncer looked him up and down. He sighed heavily. "You don't have any ID, do you? How old are you?"

"I uh..." John stammered, unsure how to answer the man's question. He had a lot to learn about street smarts. Just because he'd been in a few brawls didn't make him Jack Comer. He had to think on his feet, a moment of hesitation out here could mean trouble.

Or death. Don't forget that fun little fact John, you still don't know if you have any weaknesses yet.

"Fuck it," the bouncer said. He scruffed his Van Dyke-style mustache. "Just gimme twenty bucks."

John reached in his pockets and fumbled around, praying he still had some money left. He smiled when he pulled out a twenty. He handed it to the bouncer.

"Have a good time kid." He taped the red wristband on him. He reached out and grabbed his arm. "And don't touch the girls."

John looked at him, his pale face deathly serious. He wondered how many skulls this man cracked for people who messed with the dancers. Truth is he could give a flying fuck about the dancers, he just wanted to know where Anarchy's hide-out was. Rather than argue with this barbarian, he nodded understandingly. "Okay."

The barbarian opened the tinted-glass door and let him by. John stepped into the strip club. Music pounded from the speakers, the beat pounding his body. He walked across the black-tiled floor, taking in the lustful scenery.

Half-naked women were everywhere, hanging around the bars, dancing on the tables. Cherry-red tables with pink chairs were scattered throughout the club, and in front of each table was a miniature stage with a pole on it. Drooling men sat at the tables, getting lap dances and stuffing dollars in g-strings.

To the far right of John was a bar filled with patrons. Sleaze balls were all over the place, shouting and whistling at the girls. All the bar tenders were females dressed in only pink underwear with fish-net stockings. They didn't seem to like the customers.

Who could blame them? Some of these dudes look like

they belong on that Date Line show. Fucking predators.

"You want a dance, baby?"

John spun around when a tall woman touched his shoulder. She had soft, yellow skin with a brownish tint. He smiled at the leggy dancer and shook his head.

"Not right now, baby. Thanks anyway."

He turned and walked forward, scoping for gang members. Small cameras were all over the ceiling and in the corners of the walls. Flat-screen TVs were at the bars, showing football games and music videos. A warm hand gently touched his arm.

"Hey honey, what's your name?" A busty red-head with blue eyes turned him around.

"Jeffrey," John answered, giving her a fake name. He glanced around while she flirted with him.

"I'm Tiffany! But everyone calls me Juggys."

Yeah I can see why John thought as he caught a glimpse of her chest. He noted the southern drawl in her voice and wondered if she was from Alabama. Behind one of the stages stood two goonish bouncers dressed in black. They glared at him for a second, then looked away, surveying the spot.

"You wanna go in the champagne room?" She gestured to the strawberry-colored door in the far left corner of the club. "We'll have more privacy in there, sugah."

"No thanks."

Juggys poked her lips out and made a sad face. John ignored the other strippers who approached him and moved on. Towards the back of the club was the main attraction—a lengthy stage with pink-and-red poles. Eight strippers were up there, moving and gyrating. In front of the stage to the right was a black-and-strawberry bar.

He made his way there, moving through the sea of dancers and skimpy-dressed servers. He sat down in one of the orange chairs, battling his nerves. He'd never been to a strip club. He didn't count that time in Brazil when him and a few buddies went to a shitty bar in town, and a few rowdy drunkards paid the women to get up on the tables.

John disregarded his jitters. He flagged down the female bar tender. She walked over and he leaned in.

"What'll you have?" she asked, shouting over the music.

He pulled out a ten. "Jack n' Coke. Hey listen I'm looking for a buddy of mine, maybe you heard of him. Priest?"

The girl stared at him, her light-blue eyes wary. Her arms were sleeved out with tattoos. Her bottom lip and nose were pierced, the black rings adding a strange exoticness to her. She glanced away and made his drink.

"Sorry," she said, sliding it to him, "can't help you."

Fucking liar John thought as he slid her the cash. He sipped his drink and looked around the bar. Various drunkards stood around, getting slushied. Somehow he didn't think they'd be much help either, but he had to try. There had to be somebody here willing to tell him where Priest was.

John glanced to his left and saw a set of stairs leading up to a pink door. It opened, and a stoutly-built woman in a dark-pink dress stepped out. Her hair was red, dyed with pink streaks. Her face and arms were tan with a golden undertone. The thing that really stuck out about her was her eyes—they were bright-pink, like the eyes of a mythical demon.

Maybe he was imagining things, but she seemed to be staring right at him. She walked down the stairs, her oval-pointed eyes fixated on him the whole time.

That's bullshit and you know it. She ain't starin' at you, that's the alcohol talking.

He quickly turned away from her and took another greedy sip of his drink, the strong alcohol burning the back of his throat. Closing his eyes he bowed his head, ignoring the hypnotic music and trying to come up with a game plan.

"So what are you doing here all by yourself?"

John opened his eyes at the sound of the throaty voice. He glanced up to see the source...and was shocked that it was Pink Eyes who asked him the question.

Holy shit! She was looking at me. So I wasn't imagining things after all.

"Cuz I ain't got no friends," John answered, chuckling. He gulped the last of his drink and faced her. "So what's your name?"

She smiled at him. "I'm Linda. Let's go somewhere and talk."

"Listen Linda," John said, leaning back in his chair, "I think you're attractive and all, but I'm just here to find out where—"

She cut him off. "Come up to my office."

His mouth hung open, her assertiveness throwing him off. He started to reject her offer, then changed his mind. Maybe *she* knew something about where Priest and his asshole goons hung out. He had a feeling the regulars weren't going to be much help, so he got up from his chair.

John followed her up the stairs and watched her open the door. When they stepped inside her office, two husky bouncers the size of Detroit smiled at her. When they saw him they hopped up from the chairs and scowled.

"It's okay boys," she said, putting her hand up, "he's with me. Leave us alone and close the door."

They stepped back, disarmed by her words. They bowed their heads rushed out of the room like their asses were on fire. When one of them pulled the door shut she stood close to John, her warm body touching his. She had her hands on her hips and she was blocking him.

"You know it's rude to ask someone their name without giving yours."

He stared at her, her pink eyes making him squirm inwardly. She was definitely tall, even without her pink heels he guessed she was five-feet-ten, easily. He nodded.

"Your right," he said, playing along. "My name is John. Nice to meet you."

She looked him up and down, then smiled. Linda turned and walked to the back of the office where her desk was.

John walked across the plush-carpeted floor, noting the pink color. The office was impressive, about the size of a living room in a single-family home. Three paintings hung on the wall behind her desk; one painting was of a rose. The other was of a pink skeleton.

The last work of art was easily the most disturbing; it was a painting of burning, naked bodies in a cornfield. He turned away in disgust, observing the rest of the office. Directly behind Linda's desk was an oak cabinet filled with alcohol of all kinds. To the right of her desk on the wall were twenty small TVs, showing the inside and outside of the LEGZ strip club.

"Nice set-up," he said, pointing to the monitors, "I see you've got your eye on things."

"I want to know about everything that goes on," she said defensively, "I don't like to miss anything. Have a seat."

She gestured towards the red chair in front of her desk. He walked up and sat down. He noticed a plate full of cocaine on the desk, and seriously considered the fact that everyone in BayView were coke heads. He glanced to the left and saw something else he'd expect to see in Linda's office—a black cabinet full of porn.

"Help yourself," she said, pushing the plate of coke towards him.

"No thanks," he said, appreciating the generous offer, "not my thing."

She looked at him with a strange expression. "I didn't think it would be."

After a few more tense seconds of her uncomfortable stare she finally made herself a line, and took a hit. She wiped her nose and turned to the expensive liquor cabinet. "How about a drink?"

He decided to accept, it probably wouldn't look good if he kept turning her down. "Yeah I'll take one."

She pulled out a bottle of Poitin and two tall glasses. She filled them to the top and handed him one. He stood up as she came around the desk to him.

"Cheers," she said, toasting him.

Probably not after I drink this shit.

He mirrored her actions as she put the glass to her mouth. They tilted their heads back and drank the bitter-tasting liquid until it was gone. They slammed their glasses down, their eyes watering, the horrible alcohol burning their throats and insides like fire.

Linda wiped her nose and eyes again. She moved over to the window that overlooked the club downstairs. "So I saw you with my girls down there. You ignored them all. What's the matter, you don't like them?"

"No," John said, struggling to answer her, "it's…not that. I'm looking for sah, something else."

Linda pulled the curtains, closing off the window. She turned around and walked to him.

She can obviously recover faster than I can. Must be used to that shitty drink.

"I know." She pressed her body against his and wrapped her arms around his neck. "Maybe I can help you."

John stared into Linda's eyes, her expression lustful. He could sense where this was going, she clearly misunderstood him.

"What I'm looking for is information."

"Mmm hmm," she said, obviously not listening to him.

The spinning in his head stopped, and he no longer felt like it was going to explode. "I'm looking for a friend of mine; Michael Priest."

She stopped smiling. Her expression turned cold

within a blink of an eye. She let go of him and walked to her desk.

"I'm also looking for Trash and Psycho. You know them?"

She walked around her desk and put the Poitin inside the liquor cabinet. "Why do you want to know about them?"

"No reason. Just want to know where I can find—"

"Why!" she exploded, her face turning dark.

Suddenly the friendly atmosphere around them got real tense, real fast. Linda looked pissed...evil, in fact. He'd been around a lot of criminals in the past few days, and had been able to read into how wicked some people were. But *this* was completely different. She didn't even look like the same person anymore, it was like some malevolent force had taken over her body.

Definitely not the lustful Linda I'd met just a few minutes ago.

"Okay then," John said. He backed slowly to the door. "Well listen it was great meeting you and all, but I have to get going! Hey thanks for the drink."

She stood still, like some soul-less zombie out of a horror movie. Her pink eyes were now slits, watching him, following his every move.

"Well hey, we gotta do this again some time!" He kept trying to put her on as he inched towards the door.

Again, no answer, just that soul-less stare. Out of nowhere she bent down, and for a second he thought she'd fell. In a flash she was on her feet again, holding an M-16 in her hands.

"Ah, shit!"

Rat-tat-tat-tat-tat!

John hit the floor as she tore the office up with the M-16. She yelled like some primal beast as she swept the rifle from side to side, decorating the floors and walls with bullets. He could hear the music being cut downstairs, then screaming.

From the sounds of it people were running out of the club.

Linda's gun clicked dry. She glanced down at the deadly weapon and grunted with rage. John opened his eyes and jumped to his feet. As she glared at the empty gun he flew across the room and kicked it out of her hands.

"What do you know about Priest?" He snapped. He grabbed her by her arms and shook her. "What about Trash? Psycho? Answer me, goddammit!"

She stared at him, her round eyes expressionless. Without warning Linda balled her fists up and punched him hard in the jaw. He stared at her, shocked by the ferociousness of the blow. Before he could react she kicked him in the chest, sending him flying backwards.

He crashed to the floor, stunned. Lying on his back he stared at the ceiling, wondering what in hell just happened. He heard something metal being flicked out.

John scrambled to his knees and forced himself from the floor. He stood on shaky legs, trying to recover from having the wind knocked out of him. Though his healing abilities were remarkable, it didn't change the fact that he could still feel pain. He looked up and glanced towards the desk, shocked to see that Linda had disappeared.

Dark, heavy breathing filled his ears as he realized something dreadful…she was standing behind him.

He spun around and was greeted by a switchblade being swung at his face. He ducked instinctively, catching flashes of her wild face as she attacked him.

"Yaaaaaaaa!"

Her animalistic yelling made his skin crawl. He ran backwards, dodging her swipes. He crashed into her desk and fell back, knocking the plate of coke to the floor. He sat up fast, catching a glimpse of her rushing towards him.

Linda raised the knife over her head and brought it down to stab him, but he reached out and grabbed her wrist. She was surprisingly strong, and for a second, thought she would actually cut him.

"What the fuck!" John struggled with her as the knife got dangerously closer to his chest. "Linda…stop! Get a hold of yourself!"

But it was no use. There was no reasoning in her hateful eyes. It was like she didn't hear or understand him. The only thing she understood was kill. His arms shook as he fought with her, the panic gripping him.

John squirmed away from the desk and let go of her wrist. He ducked out of the way as she lunged past him, stabbing the desk violently. He rolled to the ground and away from her as she managed to get the knife lodged in the wood.

She yanked it out of the desk and twirled wildly, searching for him. As he got to his feet she crept towards him, the knife trembling in her hand.

"All right now Linda, that's enough." John put his hands up, trying to reason with her. He really didn't want to hit her, he was trying hard not to, but if she kept this up then he might not have a choice. "Just put it down."

She didn't answer. She inched towards him, her eyes filled with utter insanity.

"Linda stop this shit now! Don't make me have to hurt you!"

She swiped at him again, trying to cut his throat. He ducked and grabbed the knife, disarming her. He swiftly got behind her and put her in a choke-hold. She grunted viciously and clawed the air.

John kept the pressure on and knelt down, bringing her to the ground. "Sssh, it's alright. Just go to sleep now. Go to sleep."

He repeated it over and over until she stopped fighting. After a few seconds she quit moving all together. He gently laid her on the floor and felt her neck for a pulse. He was happy that she still had one. Downstairs he heard the sounds of angry male voices.

BOOM! BOOM!

Shotgun blasts followed, and he knew that that was his cue to leave. He looked around the lavish office and spotted a black-painted window next to the disturbing painting. He went to the front door, satisfied that he was far enough away. He ran at top speed and dove to the window, crashing through it.

"Shiiit!" he yelled as he fell downwards, suddenly thinking this was not a smart idea.

Air left his body as he fell farther and farther down. He landed in a trash-filled dumpster, the garbage bags breaking his fall. He laid within, feeling disoriented. As he rested in the sea of filth he heard more explosive gunfire. Whatever was happening in the strip club was beginning to spill out into the streets.

No time to rest John, get the fuck outta here!

He pulled himself out of the dumpster and crouched behind it. He glanced around for any signs of running cops.

"Thank Christ," he whispered to himself when he didn't see any yet.

Across the street was an unlit alley. The fuzz would be crawling all over this place, and if he hung around any longer trying to figure out what to do, they'd find him. He sure as hell didn't want to go into the alleyway.

He sighed, knowing that he didn't have many options. It was either an escape through the alley of doom, or a nice cold jail cell for the night. He glanced around again for a few seconds, then sprinted across the street, grateful there weren't any cars around.

He bolted through the dark alleyway, hopping crates and trashcans. Glass and other debris crunched under his shoes as he maneuvered his way to freedom. Behind him the blaring police sirens were getting closer.

He bolted down the endless alleyway, the angry sirens motivating him to run faster. His heart thudded in his chest as he sprinted onward.

SEVENTEEN

FASTER.

His muscles ached and his legs burned from the strain. Thoughts of stopping entered his mind, he felt like he was going to pass out if he didn't rest.

Faster. Something dark and sizable leapt from the shadows, sailing past him, turning his blood to ice in a split second. He tensed at the sight of it—

—and was relieved when he realized it was a black cat, out for a late night prowl. But he didn't stop running.

Faster! *Come on dammit, run faster!* he thought angrily. His body felt like rubber and his head buzzed with dizziness, making the hellish run all the more unbearable. Fearing the police sirens he ran and ran…until he didn't hear them anymore.

John stopped and cocked his head to the side. He stood like a statue and strained to hear for them, not trusting the silence. A full minute passed—

—but he still didn't hear them. He'd ran so fast and long that he'd actually gotten far away from the threat of the cops. He moved on.

How long is this damn alleyway? he wondered as he crept forward. A feint summer wind blew through the broken windows of the buildings, the gusts turning into night whispers.

He flinched as more wind blew through his hair and whistled within the streets. Dripping water from a busted drainpipe echoed throughout the alleyway, the sound somehow magnified.

Cursing the darkness he glanced around frantically. He was between two abandoned housing complexes. He wanted to get out. He wanted to be away from this horrid alley, and was seriously starting to think that getting bagged by the cops would've been better.

Cut it out, soldier. Be where you are. Don't go soft now, just concentrate on getting back to Summerville.

He trembled and hurried on, the adrenaline making his teeth chatter. Funk and rotten sewage wafted through the air, confirming his suspicions that the buildings around him were abandoned.

John took another step…and stumbled when something hard struck him in the back of his head. Confused, he tried to turn around…and suddenly he was off his feet. It felt like ginger ale was in his skull and he found it hard to stand.

He laid on the ground, not remembering the fall. Cold hands reached out and grabbed him; and suddenly he was being dragged into one of the buildings. He couldn't see who was dragging him but he knew it was two people…he could hear them breathing as they dragged him up wooden, decrepit steps.

The air reeked of piss and decay, the scent of it overpowering, making the back of his throat lock. Through the confusion he heard giggling. Creepy, insidious giggling.

The room he was forced into was dimly lit, but he still couldn't get a good look of his surroundings. Blurry shapes was all he could see.

"Hee, hee, hee!" the mysterious giggler cackled. "Put him in the chair. *Put him in the fucking chair!*"

The sinister voice was male, the sound of it making John's teeth chatter. He felt himself being slammed into a wooden seat. He grabbed his stomach and doubled over, fearing that he would blow chunks from the pain and stink.

Slowly John's vision came into focus. The blurry man

in front of him was sitting in a chair, facing him, leering at him. It was still too dark to see him clearly but he could feel him smiling…he was in trouble. He bowed his head and doubled over again.

"Sit up," the man whispered, his voice eerily smooth. "Sit—sit up! Sit him the fuck up! *Now!*"

A strong hand slapped him in the back of his head. Someone grabbed his shoulders and forced him up, then someone else slid a table in between him and the angry giggler.

A rusty light swung from the ceiling, the ancient bulb doing a shitty job of illuminating the room…and then he saw him. The evil giggler's face.

John glared at the long-haired freak sitting across from him. The man reached inside of his Army jacket and pulled out a lighter. He lit the cigarette in his mouth, the small flame showing his unshaven face. The man scratching his stubble grinned wickedly, exposing his yellow, rotten teeth.

"Why did you grab me you fucking hobgoblin?" John snapped.

"My name is Night Wish. What's yours?" the wicked man asked. John ignored his question and glanced around.

He was in a room that looked like it'd been hit by a tornado. Dead rats and broken furniture covered the floors. Blood and graffiti were smeared everywhere, and he was positive that whoever had lived here had checked out a long time ago.

Behind him stood a man with a sawed-off shotgun, dressed in black from head-to-toe. A white clown mask covered his face.

Standing next to the masked man was another burly individual, also dressed darkly. His orange face was covered in burns, giving his skin an unreal, rubbery appearance. His beady eye was black and marble-sized…the other one had been burned away, a dark hole in its place. He reached inside of his trench coat and pulled out an automatic pistol.

"Look at me when I talk to you!" Night Wish exploded, the smooth sound of his voice suddenly raspy.

John flinched. He slowly turned around and met his gaze evenly.

"Look at *me*. Look…thaaat's it. Look at me."

When John saw his eyes he decided that it would be a bad idea to piss this guy off. His wide eyes were blood-shot, the left one twitching wildly. From the looks of his long, wild, matted hair he guessed that it had been awhile since he had seen a bath. His skin had a sickly tint to it, the sight of it making his presence more uncomfortable.

"What is your naaame."

"John," he answered, shifting uncomfortably. The nausea had finally passed.

Night Wish giggled. He blew a cloud of smoke in John's face and stared at him wickedly. He chewed on his dirty fingernails, then scratched the quarter-sized sore on his neck.

"Now can you tell me why you and your friends snatched me up?"

Night Wish's giggling rose to high-pitched laughter. He cackled like a sick old man and cocked his head back, obviously finding more humor in the question than anyone else.

What the fuck is wrong with this man? He doesn't even seem human. God, what have I gotten myself into now? I shoulda' stayed at April's place tonight.

"What are you doing out here at this ungodly hour?" Night Wish asked, stifling a snicker. "Don't you know how dangerous it is to be out at this time of night? Hmmm?"

"No. I guess not."

"At this moment there are p-people being robbed!" he stuttered. He picked at the sore on his neck as he spoke. "There are people. People being shot! It's not even safe to walk the streets at night. Can you believe that?"

"No," John answered sarcastically, shaking his head. "I find that hard to believe."

"Shut up! Shut the fuck up!" Night Wish erupted. His face twisted into a freakish mask of anger as he hopped up. He reached inside of his jacket and pulled out a Colt Python Magnum.

He ran around the table and grabbed John's collar and shook him violently. He shoved the Colt in his face and screamed at him, the smell of nicotine and influence thick on his rotten breath.

"Don't you mock me, you piece of fuck! Don't you ever make fun of me I'll kill you!"

John trembled, noting how dangerously tight his finger was around the trigger. The gun shook violently in his hands and he realized that the slightest twitch would set the hammer off.

"I'll shoot you, you motherfucker!" Night Wish hissed, spit flying through his teeth. "I'll shoot the fucking blood out your fucking body and *bathe* in it! You motherfucker!"

"Okay I'm sorry! Look I wasn't making fun of you, but I'm sorry. I, um, it was stupid of me to say that. Honest to God, I would never try to offend—"

"Shut the fuck up! I oughta shoot you right now, you dippy motherfucker! Think yous can play with me, hah?"

John closed his eyes and shook his head. "No, no of course not."

"Think yous can play me?"

"No."

"You wanna play games with me, cocksucker? You wanna play?"

He glanced up at him. His throat went dry when he saw the wild look in his eyes. "No!"

"You wanna play? Well fuck you!"

John closed his eyes. "Don't!"

BLAM!

He clenched his teeth and felt his blood go cold at the sound of the shot. Wondering why he didn't feel any pain he opened them...and saw Night Wish standing in front of him, his smoking Colt raised in the air. He'd blown a hole in the ceiling. He cracked up laughing and pointed at him.

"You shoulda seen your face!" He ran around the room, his oily jacket fluttering. "I got ya you prick! Hey Fire Bug did ya see him? Clown Face, was he shakin?"

Great John thought bitterly. *The one with the mask on must be Clown Face. How original.*

Night Wish cackled louder, smiling at everyone. No one else was laughing.

BLAM!

He fired off another shot to the ceiling, enjoying the lunacy. In a fit of what seemed like joy and psychosis he spun wildly and squeezed the trigger.

BLAM! BLAM! BLAM!

Everyone ducked as the aimless bullets tore into the walls. He turned to the window and shot the glass out, the shattering sound deafening.

He wiped his nose with the back of his sleeve and licked his lips nervously. His entire body was shaking with glee as he slowly walked to John. His smile melted when he glanced at the floor where he'd dropped his cigarette. A dot-like flame was burning on the floor, and suddenly his ghoulish eyes went vacant.

"Do you like fire, John?" Night Wish asked.

He sat still and shook his head. "I'm not sure what you mean."

Night Wish kept staring at the flame. His eyes widened as he spoke.

"You see fire fascinates me, John...and terrifies me, too. Let me tell you a story about a young boy. He couldn't have been no more than, eight years old. You see this boy's father was a real piece of shit, a gambler, and he'd smack his son around when he'd get a few drinks in him.

"Well needless to say, the little boy got tired of this motherfucker hittin' on him all the time! So you know what he did? One night, when his dear old dad was fast asleep, God bless his drunken soul…the boy went into the kitchen and grabbed the gasoline from under the sink. He grabbed a match, and he went into his father's room. His father's rooooom!

"And guess what that little boy did? He, he poured the gas all over his dear old dad's bed. And he lit the match…and then he set him on *fire!* And he watched him burn. He watched him burn! He watched him *burn!*"

John listened in horror and watched Night Wish shake; he shook with an incomprehensible fury like none he'd ever known.

"Burn burn!" he shrieked, grabbing his hair. "Burn burn! Burn buuurrrn!"

Tears streamed down his face as he closed his eyes. He spun around wildly, yelling the word burn over and over again. The mad man hung his head and stopped yelling. He stayed quiet for a full agonizing minute, the silence unnerving to John. The tiny flame flickered suddenly, and went out. He raised his head and stared at him.

"You like games, Johnny Boy?" the lunatic asked. He wiped his sweaty hand on his blue jeans.

"Huh?"

"Games! You know, do you like games?" he reached inside of his pocket and pulled out a bullet.

John tensed more, not liking where this was going. "Uh, yeah. Crossword puzzles mostly."

"Fuck that!" he snapped, loading the Colt with the bullet. "I know a better game."

John flinched at the sound of his voice. It was child-like, and…scary. He watched as he sat and pulled up closer to the table. His glassy, innocent eyes were rolling around in his sockets, scanning the room out of paranoia.

"Ever play Russian Roulette?" he asked. His eyes narrowed, and his voice had turned smooth and sinister again; his real voice.

The man's a schizophrenic John thought uneasily. *I've heard of this before. I always thought it was bullshit, but it's true. This condition is real.*

"This is an old-fashioned Magnum John," he whispered, "A Colt Python. See the handle there? They don't make em' like this no more! I got this off a guy after I...well, it doesn't matter how I got it, does it? It's mine now."

He said a prayer in his head as the whack job went on about his Colt. Behind him he felt Clown Face press the sawed-off barrel to the back of his head.

"Know how to play?" Tears streamed out of Night Wish's face as he grinned wider. "It's simple, really. This gun can hold six bullets in the chamber there...but there's only one. One bullet, Johnny. Now we both take turns pullin' the trigger, see? Now you take this fuckin' gun and put it to your head, and squeeze. And if you don't blow your brains out yous pass it to me, and it's my turn! Whoever lives is the winner."

John's stomach knotted. He swallowed hard, not liking his new friend's game. "I think I'll pass."

Night Wish glared at him, his eyes narrowed lines. Fire Bug lurched around the table and stood behind the crazed gunman. He stared at him mutely and raised his automatic pistol, aiming it at John's face.

"You see you're going to play, Johnny boy," Night Wish hissed. He slammed the Colt down and pushed it across the splintered table. "Now let's begin. You first."

John sighed heavily, unable to control his nerves. He caught a whiff of Night Wish's body odor. His skin stunk of illegal influence, and something familiar; disease. It was the smell of blood and death, and it was oozing out of his pores.

Don't leave me, Lord John thought. Sweat poured off

of his face as he picked up the Colt and put it to his temple. He closed his eyes and pulled the trigger.

Click!

At the sound of the dry click he jumped and opened his eye. To his amazement his head was still on his shoulders.

"Yeah!" Night Wish cheered. He banged the table with his fist and roared with laughter. "Yeah, Johnny!"

He sighed with relief and let the gun slip through his fingers. The fact that he didn't blow his brains out brought him no comfort; they still had *five* turns to go.

"Yeah! Yeah! Yeah!"

Night Wish snatched up the Colt and put it to his head, pulling the trigger immediately. There was no hesitation. No pause. He genuinely did not give a shit if he lived or died. He slammed it down and slid it across the table, a look of triumph plastered on his psychotic face. He reached for the gun, ready to take his turn.

"Where you from, Johnny?" he asked. He reached out and put his hand over the cannon of death.

"Los Angeles," he lied.

He grinned his rotten-mouthed grin. "So yous from Los Angeles, hah? Well you're a long ways away from home, ain't ya?"

He didn't answer.

"I knew you weren't from here. What in the world are yous doin' all the way out here?"

John tried to stop the butterflies in his stomach. "Just taking care of some personal business, that's all."

"That's a crock of shit. Well it don't matter now, does it? Yous in the wrong place at the wrong time. Now I'm gonna learn ya a lesson."

"Where are you from?" John asked, raising his eyebrow. He couldn't be sure, but Night Wish sounded like he was from the east coast. It was obvious that he wasn't from the wonderful city of BayView either, his out-of-town dialect seemed to pronounce itself at random, changing the way he said things. He silently wondered how long he'd been in these mean streets. "I'm just curious, you don't sound like you're—"

"Shut up!" Night Wish yelled. He smacked him across the face with the Colt. "Shut the fuck up! Why do yous wanna know where I'm from, hah? You a cop? Are you a fucking cop?"

John grabbed his throbbing face as he shook his head. He saw infinite stars, the vicious blow from the butt of the gun scrambling his mind. Night Wish grabbed a fistful of his shirt and pressed his gun to his temple.

"I'll kill you, ya son-of-a-bitch! *I'll* kill you!"

John frowned up at him. *But it's your turn, you asshole!*

"You're a worthless maggot, you fucking piece of shit! You had no business being out here, you motherfucker, you. Now you're gonna die for it goddammit. Die! Die! Die! Now tell me how worthless yous are. You fucking fuck! Say it."

He shielded his face and flinched away from the gun. Every fiber of his being wanted to get up and fight, to knock the gun out of his hands; he chose not to, and thought of a way to stall him as he played his twisted game. "Alright."

"Say it," he snarled.

"Alright, man. I'm worthless."

"Say it!" Night Wish yelled.

"I'm fuckin' worthless! Okay?"

"Say it again, you motherfucker! Say it louder!"

"I'm worthless, worthless, worthless!"

"I'll kill ya…I'll kill ya!" He pulled the trigger. *Click!*

"Ha ha, haaa! I like this game!" Night Wish bellowed. "I like it! You want to know why?"

He put the Magnum to his head and pulled the trigger…and a dry click echoed throughout the wretched room.

"Because somebody always dies, hah? That's why I

love it! But the question is…who's it gonna be?"

Night Wish put the gun to his head. He glanced around at them, his eyes the size of golf balls. Fire Bug's face was blank, his expression deader than a two-day-old stiff's. "Who's it gonna be?"

John shrugged. "I don't know man."

"Get the fuck outta here!" He scowled at him and pointed the Magnum at his face. "You're not supposed to know. You kiddin' me?"

Clown Face grunted behind him, jabbing the sawed-off painfully into his back. As the tension in the room thickened his mind raced; he had to get away from these goons. Fast.

"I got two shots left in this gun, my friend. And it's also my turn! See this next shot could probably kill me, or be an empty chamber. Which means I could *A*—shoot you and skip my turn, *B*—take my turn like I'm supposed to. Hah? Or *C*—shoot you in the fuckin' balls!"

John flinched inwardly at the last option. Somehow he didn't think Mr. trigger happy would choose option *B*. As he put the gun to his head he racked his brain for a plan of escape.

"Now the game's taken an interesting turn, no? Because now you don't know what the fuck I'm gonna do! All yous knows is that you could be leavin' here tonight without your head—or your balls!"

He looked at the ceiling and laughed, the sound of his insane humor chilling. He stopped giggling and stared down at him, the smile gone from his face.

"Or maybe I'll keep my word, hah? And take my turn over here. Either way it's time to find out. Say goodnight, Johnny boy. Say goodnight."

Time slowed to a crawl. The swinging, rusty lamp resonated in his ears, and suddenly every one and thing else disappeared as his vision turned dream-like, and there were only two people left in the room—him and Night Wish.

"Say goodnight, Johnny boy. Say goodnight."

John's body shook as he tried one last time to think of something quick...and then he wasn't thinking anymore.

"Fuck you!" John hollered.

He grabbed Night Wish's trigger hand and hopped up, knocking the table over in the process. He snatched the Colt away from him and aimed upwards at the light; the last thing he saw in the room was the sick man's surprised face—

BLAM!

He blew the light out of the ceiling. It shattered, and before it could hit the ground he ducked—and then the shooting started.

BOOM!

Sounds of the sawed-off thundered in his ears. A muffled cry filled the room as Fire Bug let loose with his automatic.

John heard another garbled cry as he blindly ran forward in the dark room, guessing that it was Clown Face this time...and then he heard screaming. High-pitched screaming, a voice he didn't recognize—

Jesus Christ, who is that?

—and the screaming changed. Deeper. It turned deeper until it was a frightening rumble, like the Loch Ness monster itself had been shot.

Gun blasts filled the room, the flashes briefly showing him what he was searching for.

The window!

Still crouching he bolted for it, the frightening sounds of screaming and fighting filling the air. He dove through the window, flailing his arms, and fell downwards to darkness, unaware of how high he was up and where the ground was. For the second time tonight he plummeted.

"Ah fuck!" John yelled. He was finally on the ground.

He landed on his shoulder, cracking it painfully on the pavement. Unbearable pain exploded within him, and suddenly he felt grateful. Grateful knowing that his shattered shoulder would heal…but it still hurt.

Struggling to his feet he could already feel his body healing itself, liquefying the agony. He quickly searched the ground for the Colt. Unable to find it he realized that he must have dropped it in the room.

"John!"

Startled, he glanced up at the eerie housing complex. The man shouting his name was Night Wish; the man of a thousand voices.

"I will find yooooooooou!"

He shuddered at the abominable yelling. Gun blasts and screaming spilled out of the broken room above, fueling his need to get ghost. "Not in this life time," he mumbled. "Dickhead."

John sprinted away, leaving the chaos behind him.

EIGHTEEN

JOHN BOOKED THROUGH THE TUNNELS OF KingStreet, desperately trying to get back to Summerville. The streets would be crawling with cops because of the LEGZ thing. He didn't feel like answering questions, and more importantly he didn't feel like getting picked up, either. As he ran up the stairs he wondered why the shooting had started in the first place.

What really bothered him was why he'd been so careless. The Linda situation should have been handled differently. If he'd been more street-savvy she probably wouldn't have gone off like that.

Once again I failed because of not using street smarts. Lesson learned.

He continued to beat himself up as he ran out of the tunnels. He hurried through Montbello Street, scanning the area for danger. There was a man leaning against the flickering light post ahead, smoking crack. Without warning the man dropped his pipe and collapsed.

John bolted towards him and knelt down beside him. His eyes rolled into the back of his head and he shook violently. Unsure of what to do he grabbed the man's hand as his seizure got worse.

Spit bubbled from his mouth and darkened the collar of his t-shirt. His blue jeans were torn, and John was amazed that he didn't even have any shoes on. The bearded man stopped shaking and laid still.

John glanced at his sun-burned face. He reached out and touched his neck, trying to find a pulse. He tried again, frowning.

Damn.

John sighed and closed the man's eyes. He stood and moved on, filled with sadness, but unable to do anything. He didn't want to call anyone and tell them that some random person had overdosed right in front of him. Besides, it was too late for him anyway.

And plus the cops might try to blame me for it. Who the hell knows? Either way I can't afford to take that chance dammit, I just can't.

He hurried down the street again. An uneasy feeling bubbled in his stomach. He frowned and turned around, having the strangest feeling he was being followed. Behind him about forty feet away was a raggedy-dressed man with a pipe in his mouth. He took a hit off it, and though it was dark, John could've sworn the shadowy figure was looking at him.

John quickly glanced away from him and crossed the street to Riverside Avenue. He gazed forward, trying to think of the easiest way to get to Summerville without taking Montbello. He looked behind him again, surprised to see that there were two crack heads following him.

He made sure to keep the same pace without seeming too obvious that he was rushing to get away from them. As he walked down the long avenue a thousand thoughts raced through his head about what he could do. After the fight with Linda he was no longer confident that he was invincible. She'd almost stabbed him in the heart.

And I don't know what these muthafuckas want. I'm almost positive they don't want to ask me for a light. Now is not the time to find out if I have a weakness, if they have any weapons on them I don't wanna risk fighting with them.

Maybe he was being too paranoid. Perhaps it was just coincidence that the two men behind him were headed in a different direction, and they just happen to be taking the same sidewalk. He casually scratched the back of his neck and turned around again.

Four crack heads.

He turned forward and walked slightly faster, not happy at the increase of people behind him. Though most of the light posts were out he could have sworn one of them was glaring at him. He rubbed his chin and glanced behind him.

Six crack heads following me now.

John turned forward and ran down Riverside. There was no mistaking it, they were after him. Footsteps thundered behind him as he ran off the avenue and cut through a dark alley, dodging discarded shopping carts, crushing beer cans and glass bottles. At the end of the alley was a brick wall, and only two ways to go; left, or right.

He chose right and hauled ass, catching a glimpse of a building up ahead. A huge sign that red Sammy's Warehouse in red-and-white letters stood atop of the building. He ran down the deserted alley.

The warm night air whipped past him as he booked onwards, pumping his arms and legs wildly. He made it to the warehouse and collapsed against the building's wall. His heart thudded in his chest as he fought to control his erratic breathing. He was happy that he'd managed to outrun the fiends.

When his breathing returned to normal he walked towards the back of the warehouse. The sound of his own heartbeat pumped in his ears, making his head ache. He turned at the corner of the warehouse and walked behind it—

—and froze dead in his tracks at the terrifying sight in front of him; hundreds of fiends staring at him with glassy eyes.

Oh, great…it's Night Of The Living Crack Heads, and I'm the main star.

Three of the dope fiends pushed their way through the crowd and rushed him, attacking him without provocation. One of them stowed him in his eye, catching him off guard.

John put his fists up and blocked the other attacks, knocking two of them out with hooks. He set the third one up with the jab, then threw an over-hand-right, breaking his chin, sending him to the Sandman's lair. He glanced up and saw the Panaca Heights projects behind the mob of dope fiends. The projects were his only escape, but getting through the fiends would be a miracle.

A large junkie wearing a red football jersey, business slacks, and white tennis shoes emerged from the crowd. The man's yellow hair was wild, and it looked like it'd been a long time since he'd seen a shower.

He charged at John, throwing wild haymakers, not landing a single one. He ducked the last haymaker and upper-cut the man in his face, splitting his chin open. Blood gushed from his open chin, staining the man's jersey as he crashed forward into a group of trashcans, knocking them over noisily.

The mob obviously didn't appreciate him beating up one of their friends. They turned more hostile, hurling insults at him.

Suddenly Michael Priest appeared. The hollering stopped abruptly at his presence. The crowd of dope addicts parted down the middle like the Red Sea did for Moses. He clutched a lead pipe in his hands, glaring at John.

"Well, well, well…as I live and fucking breathe." Priest smiled hatefully, his blue eyes glimmering. "Little John, what on earth are you doing out at such a dangerous hour? You should be home tucked away under the covers."

"Cut the shit, Priest!" John exploded. "Did you kill my friend Charlie? Was it you?"

"Kill? Why John, whatever do you mean?"

He ignored his taunting. "Was it Trash?"

"Where are you staying these days, my friend?"

"Or was it that idiot Psycho? You might as well cut it the fuck out and tell me. I'm not going to stop until I find out."

Priest made tisking noises with his mouth and closed

his eyes, shaking his head. "You know, you really shouldn't have come out here tonight. You realize that, don't you?"

He frowned and shook furiously, ready to tear him limb from limb. "I'll find out if you killed him, you know. I may not get you tonight, but I'm going to keep coming after you until I find the answers...I won't stop."

Priest stopped smiling, his face turning ice-cold. "You're gonna die tonight."

The mob of druggies kept quiet as the two of them stood in silence, glowering at each other. Time itself seem to stop as the stand-off continued. No one made a move. Finally, Priest tossed the lead pipe to a burly junkie.

"Listen up! I promise each and every man here free crack all night! Do you hear me? On one condition...this asshole dies. I want his fucking body chopped in half, and I want it brought to *me!* Did you all get that?"

The crack heads trembled with glee, not believing the glorious offer. They buzzed amongst themselves, glancing around at each other with wide, glassy eyes.

"Free crack!"

Priest glared at John. After he hollered his last words he turned and walked through the excited mob, then disappeared to the projects. The crack heads wasted no time. They scoured the ground, arming themselves with bricks, rocks, and broken bottles.

Whack!

John stumbled forward when something hard had smashed into the back of his head. He spun around to see his attacker, the stars in his vision making it difficult. The brawny man Priest had tossed the lead pipe to was in front of him, ready to strike again. He growled at him, his camouflage pants and sneakers filthy.

He swung at John again, and missed him miserably. He snatched the lead pipe away from him and smashed him up side his head, killing him before he hit the floor. Behind him a fiend in a jogging suit rushed him with a glass bottle. He hit him in the body four times, then clobbered him in the forehead, crushing his face to a bloody pulp.

    John cocked back the pipe in his hands like a baseball player, getting ready to bash the hell out of the rest of them. Sharp pain exploded within him as a brick slammed into his back. He spun around and knocked the brick-thrower backwards as other fiends rushed him, stabbing him with broken bottles. One of them stabbed him deep, puncturing his lung. He coughed up a wad of blood and spun around fiercely.

    Swinging the pipe he continued to slay the horde of crack heads, smashing them with the deadly weapon, killing a few of them, crushing their skulls. Infinite fiends flew through the air as he swung and swung.

    John lost all track of time. He kept swinging until there was no one fighting him. Out of breath he lowered the heavy pipe and gazed downwards. Hundreds of unconscious crack heads littered the ground. Amazed, he crept through the collapsed mob, glancing at them, unable to believe he'd slain so many by himself.

    He noticed one fiend in a red break-dancing outfit, the blue stripes running up and down his sleeves and pants. His shoes looked like something out of the nineteen-eighties, and his blonde hair was wild. The man was down for the count, crack pipe still in his hand.

    As John stood he had a moment of clarity; he was invincible. Indestructible. *Untouchable.* Nobody could fuck with him, he'd been stabbed enough to die a hundred times. But he didn't. He was an invincible killing machine, and there was nothing that anyone could do to stop his wrath.

    John dropped the lead pipe and ran off. Behind him, the crack head with the break dancing clothes awoke. Confused, he glanced around for a second. He took a hit off his crack pipe, then passed out again.

NINETEEN

APRIL MOVED BRISKLY IN THE EMPTY TUNNELS, anxious to get home. She couldn't stop thinking about Lang. She was frustrated by how mulish he was, and at the same time not surprised. She'd expected him to be like that, trying to reason with him was like talking to a brick wall.

A gust of wind blew through her shoulder-length hair. Newspapers and candy wrappers flew into her face as she walked. She loathed being in the tunnels late at night, and suddenly wished that she'd waited to visit Lang until the weekend.

A wanted poster caught her attention. She went over to the dirty wall and stood in front of it, staring at the poster. Waves of antipathy washed over her.

Fucking creeps, I can't stand it anymore! While the police are sitting on their behinds these assholes are tearing this city apart. Doesn't anyone care?

Heavy footsteps echoed behind her as she stared at the poster. She turned around and saw nothing…then caught a glimpse of a man in the distance, walking towards her. A black bandana was wrapped around his head, and she could see tufts of his mohawk sticking out of it. Another bandana was wrapped around his face, and she could already tell that he was one of those Punk assholes.

April clutched her purse strap tightly and wondered how long she'd been standing there. *Long enough, you idiot* she thought. She turned and started speed-walking towards the tunnel exit, her heels clicking loudly.

She walked faster. Icy panic spilled within her when

she heard the creep behind her walking faster as well. She moved quicker, practically running this time, realizing yet again that the person behind her was doing the same. She took off, cursing the damn heels for making it hard to run.

She staggered clumsily as one of the heels broke, making her roll her ankle. She shrieked and kicked it off, trying to ignore the blinding panic building inside of her. A strong hand wrapped around her arm, turning her fear into all-out shock.

"Good evening, bitch!" the man rasped into her ear. "Nice night for a walk, ain't it?"

April cried out and struggled to get away, but his grip was too strong. His breath was sour and reeked of alcohol and drugs, the stench making her queasy.

"Fuckin' spoiled little miss bitch decided to take a nice little stroll, eh? Well fuck you! Gimme your money, I know you got it!"

She shook with terror when she heard his croaking, frog-like voice. It was the same voice she'd heard a couple of nights ago outside of the Sun Tree.

"Ya-you!" she said, stuttering. "You killed Charlie, you're the one!"

His steel grip tightened. "You're dead!"

He reached out and choked her, holding her at arms length. She beat his arms and tried to call out for help. He brutally shook her and she could feel the life being strangled out of her. Her mind raced as she tried to think of a way to fight him before it was too late.

April kicked him hard in the balls. He let go of her instantly and grabbed his crotch, groaning. He turned away from her and she ran over to him. She kicked him again, this time in the ass, losing her shoe in the process. The man fell to the floor and curled up in the fetal position.

She grabbed her purse and ran to the exit. Behind her the bandana Punk hollered psychotically, the sound of his voice making her run faster. She made it to the top of the stairs...and paused at the sight of the creepiest man she'd ever seen.

A tall man with thick glasses and brown, curly hair stood in front of her. He was dressed in a green-striped polo shirt and wrinkled blue jeans. His brown shoes were stained and battered. His bulging eyes were wide, and her internal alarms went crazy when he took a step towards her.

She didn't hesitate. She hit him in the face with her purse, knocking his glasses off. She pulled out her can of mace and sprayed Creepy Man in the eyes. He screamed and knocked the can out of her hands, then covered his pallid face. She kicked Creepy down the stairs. Ignoring the wailing men she turned and hauled ass away.

April took off into the night, ignoring the pain in her feet.

John slammed April's door shut and leaned against it. Head spinning he was intoxicated with power. He ran into the living room and spun around wildly, almost knocking the TV over. He bounced around the living room, throwing jabs at the air, jacked up for another fight.

He stopped shadowboxing after a few minutes and stumbled over to the curtains. He opened them and stared out at the city lights. He stood a moment, excited, drinking in the view of the perilous city.

I can conquer the world and nobody would be able to stop me...but no. No, no, that's not what I want. I'm here to find Charlie's killer and end his life. Then I'm going to take down Anarchy. I'm going to destroy the Punks once and for all, and nobody's gonna get in my way.

John didn't hear the door unlock. It took the sound of April stumbling through the front and collapsing to bring him out of his fantasy. He rushed to her.

"April? What's the matter?"

She looked up at him, her hazel eyes wide and full of tears. "They attacked me and, and I fought them. I fought them off I…they were awful but I…think I killed him. Oh, God!"

He gently grabbed her and helped her up. "Hey come on, it's okay. It's okay now."

John glanced down at her feet, noting that they were bleeding and blistered. He reassured her in a soothing voice as he helped her over to the couch.

TWENTY

JOHN HANDED APRIL MORE BANDAGES FOR HER feet as she told him more of her ordeal. He complained silently to himself, still angry about how she was trippin' earlier. She'd tried to tell him where she kept her foot pans, but she was so hysterical that he couldn't understand her. How was he supposed to know where the they were? Maybe if she'd calmed down he would've seen them in the towel cabinet, dammit.

"...and then I kicked him down the stairs and ran," April said.

John handed her a towel. "And you said he had on thick glasses, huh?"

"Yeah," she answered. He noticed that she was still shaking, but had calmed down considerably. "I'm telling you though, this was the creepiest guy I'd ever seen in my life."

"Would you recognize him again if you saw him? What about the other guy?"

She finished drying her feet and threw the towel aside. "I don't know, the other guy was covered with bandanas, I couldn't see his..."

She trailed off. Her mouth went slack and her eyes were distant. For a second she'd reminded John of a wind-up doll that ran out of juice. Suddenly her eyes widened, and she jumped up.

"The other guy! Of course, that's what I wanted to tell you! The guy with the bandanas who attacked me...when he threatened me, his voice was like gravel. It was the same voice I'd heard that night your friend was murdered. The same guy that attacked me tonight. He's the one who killed Charlie."

John stared at her, motionless. Whatever she said next fell on deaf ears, he couldn't hear her. She looked worried as she asked him something. Everything around him moved in slow motion, and for a moment he found it hard to move.

"What…did you just say?" he heard himself asking her, alarmed by the intensity of his own voice.

"I asked if you needed to sit down. You don't look so good."

"No, before that!"

She flinched at his response. He felt a strange tightness in his chest. It was like a small marble of tension had settled there. The feeling was weird and unwelcoming.

"Where did you see him?"

She gazed at him strangely. "I don't under—"

"*Where.*"

"In the tunnels, John. I told you that."

Her voice had turned soft, and for some reason he didn't like that. It pissed him off. In fact, it reminded him of how the doctor's spoke to him when he'd returned from the war, they sounded patronizing. He ran to the bathroom. He snatched the cabinet door open and grabbed his bag.

"Where are you going?" she asked from the living room.

He ignored her as he unzipped it. He pulled out the .380 pistol. This time he would make damn sure not to forget his weapons. He stormed towards the front door. April appeared in front of him, standing between him and the door.

"John what's wrong? Where…what is *that*? Where did you get that?"

He stared at her coldly. "I got somewhere to be. Get out of my way."

"Where are you going?"

He squeezed the strap of his bag. "Move."

She crossed her arms, meeting his gaze evenly. "What

are you going to do?"

"Get out the way!"

"Would you just listen to me for a second?" Her voice was all tight and funny, but she stood her ground. He was menacing right now, his anger making him look like a horrific goblin, but somehow she found the strength to confront him. "Just listen to me!"

"No you listen!" he boomed, his entire body shaking with rage. "You just told me that the man who killed Charlie attacked you in the tunnels? I need to go find him. I need to go to the goddamn tunnels and get him before he gets away. The longer I stay here arguing with you…"

"Okay, but why are you going now?" She uncrossed her arms and put them in the air. "That was over an hour ago, he's probably gone by now!"

He gritted his teeth and glared at her. That's not what he wanted to hear, but common sense was sinking in. He had to accept the fact that she was right.

"Goddammit," he said, whispering the word under his breath. He let the heavy bag slide off of his back and fall to the floor. Biting his lip he turned away from her and slowly walked to the couch.

John slumped in the cushions and gazed at the blank TV screen. The desire to go out there and blindly search for the murdering bastard was overwhelming. It seemed like the closer he got to finding the mystery man, the more obstacles popped up to stop him.

"Son-of-a-bitch," he hissed. He frowned and put the .380 on the glass coffee table.

She sat next to him. "Listen I know how you must feel. I'm frustrated too, but we have to be smart about this. You can't just go around the city blowing everyone's head off, you have to let the cops handle it. And you told me you wouldn't do anything crazy. Do you remember promising me?"

He stared at her sheepishly, then turned away from her. *Knock, knock!*

He hopped up from the couch. "Who the fuck is that?"

She stood, her expression non-chalant. She pulled her cell phone out of her pocket. "Oh yeah, that's the cops. I called them when I was running home. About time they showed up, it's been over an…"

"You called the cops?" he asked, interrupting her.

"Well yeah, of course I did. Why wouldn't I have?"

John snatched up his .380. He tip-toed over to his bag and scooped it from the floor, then headed for the door to her balcony. He turned to her, his face covered with sweat.

"Stall em'. Don't tell em' I'm here."

She stared at him, confused. "What is wrong with—"

"—and whatever you do, *don't* tell them about Charlie," he whispered.

Before she could respond he opened the door to the balcony and gently closed it. He delicately put his bag down and tucked his pistol. The sound of the door opening panicked him. He jumped over the railing and grabbed it, hanging off of the balcony.

Shit. That's all I need right now, the fucking cops! I don't want them to find Charlie's killer, then I won't be able to take care of him myself. Please keep your mouth shut in there, April. Please…

The air burned his face as it blew past him, the hot night unforgiving. He squeezed his eyes closed, wishing to God that they would just leave already. As he hung from the balcony he strained to listen.

"…you guys over an hour ago! I could have been dead by now, why does it take the police so long to…"

John could only hear bits and pieces of the conversation. For the most part all he could hear was April's voice since she was so upset. Busy night traffic bustled beneath him, the sounds of cursing and blaring car horns filling the dark sky. His heart froze in his chest as the balcony door opened.

"Where are you?"

He glanced up to see April's soft eyes staring down at his. Relieved, he pulled himself up.

"What are you doing down there?"

He pulled himself back onto the balcony and laid on the floor. "Just hangin' out."

She shook her head. "They're gone. Come back inside."

Never a moment to rest he thought. Like a punch-drunk fighter he stumbled to his feet and staggered inside. She slammed the door shut and stomped towards her room, cursing under her breath.

"Sooo, what happened?"

"I'll tell you what happened," she snapped, twirling around to face him. "The cops told me I can't go to work tomorrow! They ordered me to stay inside until they find the man who attacked me. I have to go to work, how am I supposed to earn a living if I don't work?"

She turned and walked into her room. Sounds of slamming drawers filled the air. He listened to her banging things around in her room, not sure what to say.

"I didn't tell them anything about Charlie or how the man's voice sounded. What good what it have done? They're idiots. It took them over an hour to respond to my call, they don't give a damn about this city!"

Well, at least she kept her mouth shut.

Seconds later she emerged from her bedroom. She had changed into a pair of blue yoga shorts and white tank-top. She glanced around the apartment, her eyes flashing with anger.

"I mean what am I supposed to do here, John? The police just told me to wait here for three days before going to work. That's bullshit, I don't see how that's going to catch the guy who attacked me. And even when I'm able to leave, who am I supposed to rely on for protection…them?"

She quickly walked over to him and held up one of the officer's cards. He took it from her as she ranted some more.

"I'll be honest with you—I don't feel safe in my own apartment anymore. What should I do?"

John threw the officer's card over his shoulder. He gently grabbed her arms, looking her square in the face.

"It's tough. I mean…it's tough, you know? That's all I can really say. Of course you want the police to handle this, why wouldn't you? But with all the crime going on out there, let's be realistic…they *can't*. Their hands are tied, there's no possible way for them to respond to every single crime that goes on, and look for one felon."

"I'm scared," she said, her voice sounding helpless. "I really don't know what to do."

He nodded. "Of course you're scared. You should be. Drugs are being sold, homes are being broken into, people are dying; you'd have to be inhuman not to be afraid. But I know what to do."

She didn't say a word as she studied him intently. He hated the fact that she was attacked tonight, but happy that she wasn't hurt. He never would've forgiven himself if something horrible had happened to her, and he would've slain the entire fucking area if she'd gotten killed. Glad that he had her complete attention, he continued.

"I'm not going to lie, this city is gone. We can't stop what goes down in BayView, but we can sure as hell do something about it. And we can do a hell of a lot more than the cops can."

"How?"

"I'm not going to lie to you. There's a way to handle things like this, but you're not going to like it. It involves guns, and more of what I have in this bag."

Judging by her face he could see that she didn't agree

with what he had in mind. He also noticed that she wasn't rejecting him, either.

She nodded slowly. "So what's the plan?"

John and April walked over to the couch, and sat down to prepare.

TWENTY-ONE

MICHAEL PRIEST STOOD ON THE ROOF OF the Skyline Towers and watched his underlings below. Business was good, he was on top of the world. Every crew in the city was under his control, the drug trade belonged to him; but Priest could not rejoice in his success. Not with one man causing so many problems.

Danny Boy and Trash stood behind him in silence. Psycho was there too, but he wasn't much help. The three of them had spoken in length about what to do with the problem-causer. He took another drag off his cocaine-laced cigarette.

"I want him alive," Priest said aloud to no one in particular.

"I don't think that's a good idea man," Trash said.

Priest knew he'd feel that way about it. He knew that Danny Boy would follow orders no matter what, but he'd somehow expected resistance from Trash. And as far as Psycho's opinion…well, that was a different story all together.

Psycho sat on the floor. He tied his arm off with a band to raise his veins. He slapped his arm a couple of times, then took a needle and shot heroin into his veins. His eyes rolled into the back of his head and he fell backwards, enjoying the horse.

"Come on man, let me do him!"

"No," he said after puffing on his cigarette. "I want him alive. If someone kills him that person is going to answer to me. You understand?"

Trash turned away, sulking. "Dude, he took out the strip club! Look; Linda's in jail, Panaca Heights is a ghost town, and now, he's cutting into our connection. Crack Cocaine is our bread and butter, Priest. If he takes that away from us we're finished! This kid is trouble. If we don't dust him now he's gonna fuck everything up, you just watch."

"He lives." Priest took one last, long drag of his cigarette. He flicked it over the edge, watching it fall to the ground below. He turned and looked at them.

Trash scoffed at the idea. "Okay man. Well let's just ask Psycho what he thinks about the idea. Hey Psycho, what do you think? You think we should off Soul Brotha, or let him live? Oh, you don't have an opinion? Oh, that's right, he can't speak. He's too doped up on fucking smack!"

Priest's blood-shot eyes were emotionless. He glanced at him and Danny Boy indifferently. "You let me deal with that, don't worry about Psycho. You just do what you're told."

"Fine. Fuckin' *A* man, no problem. But what are you going to do with this kid when you catch him?"

He stared at Trash for a second. "I'll deal with that, too."

Danny and Trash glanced at each other again. They headed for the stairs, then stopped and turned to Priest.

"What do you want us to do about Scottie?" Trash asked.

Priest turned away from them. He peered over the edge of the building again. Down below the Punks were selling to hundreds of fiends. He looked away from the dope slingers and stared at the blazing sky.

"Kill him."

Danny and Trash paused for a moment. They shrugged, then turned and walked down the weak stairwell. As they left Priest pondered to himself about John.

"What is this man?" he said, wondering why John Cutter hadn't died yet.

John sighed, irritated as he headed for the door. "For

the last time April, *no*. Look, I'm just going to do some more asking around, okay? I don't need you tagging along, just wait here 'til I get back."

"Well aren't you at least going to take a gun with you?" She stood by the loveseat with her arms crossed.

"Not if I'm just going to ask around. I just need to get a general idea of where to look for these guys, alright? I'm less likely to run into trouble if I do that in the daytime. Now look, don't argue with me, okay?"

She didn't answer. She stood silently, pouting as he started to leave. He glanced down at the floor and shook his head, then looked at her.

If people would just listen to me and not ask questions, things would be so much easier. Why does everything have to be so hard?

John walked to the middle of the living room and unzipped his bag on the floor. He pulled the 9-mm out, then stood and moved to her. "Have you ever used one of these?"

April shook her head, her arms still crossed. "No, never."

He reached down and put the pistol in her hands. He stood behind her, raising her arms. "I'm going to give you a crash course, then. This is the safety, okay? If it's up like this, then the gun won't fire. Push it down and you're ready for action. Safety on, safety off…on, off. Got it?"

She nodded, soaking up his instructions like a sponge.

"This is the trigger. You don't even have to pull it that hard. If some creeps' fuckin' with you, all you have to do is squeeze…and boom, no more creep. Careful, it's loaded."

He took the gun from her and put it on the coffee table, then headed for the door. Worried, he turned and glanced at her.

"You straight? Think you'll be okay using that now?"

She nodded quickly. "Uh-huh. Got it."

Yeah, right. Probably wind up shooting herself instead.

He signed inwardly, then opened the door. "Hang tight, I'll be back soon."

He ran down the stairs and away from Summerville, hoping that he didn't make a mistake by leaving her alone.

John whistled as he moved down Montbello Street, happy that he'd been able to do so without incident. The fact that he went this long without getting into a fight today was amazing. Though he considered himself born invincible he was tired of the constant run-ins with the gangs. He took Riverside and crossed the street to Freddy's Fries. He glanced down at the silver watch he'd bought from a young tuff just ten minutes ago.

Probably stole it from somewhere. That kid looked way too young to be a jeweler. Ah, well...

"Eleven AM," he said to himself. "Think I'll go into Freddy's for a burger."

"Are you the guy looking for Priest?"

John let go of the door handle and spun around. A man with a shaved head and blue eyes stood behind him. He was dressed in a black Armani suit, his blue tie matching his cufflinks and handkerchief. The sharply-dressed man looked like he was only in his twenties.

"Who are you?" he asked him warily.

"The name's Sedgewick," the man said. He stepped forward with his hand out. "I'm a friend of Mr. Lang's. I heard about Charlie. Please, accept my condolences."

John shook his hand, but stayed on point. He studied his body language, ready to knock his head off if he so much as blinked wrong.

"You said you could take me to Priest?"

"Yes sir," Sedgewick said. He nodded towards the street. "I can take you to his hide-out."

"Let me ask you something. Why are you helping me? Every person I've asked about the gang so far has tried to blow my head off."

He shrugged gloomily. "I'm just a concerned citizen, that's all. I'm tired of all this violence, and I want it to end."

"Can you take me to Anarchy's hide-out now?"

The sharp dresser nodded. "Follow me."

John followed him as he walked away from Freddy's. They jogged twenty blocks down, then turned left at a deserted alley. He led him to an abandoned building.

Four Spikers with mohawks materialized from behind the ominous-looking building. John frowned, puzzled.

"Hey, what's going on here?"

He turned around. Before he could ask anything else Sedgewick had taken off running. The stranger he'd trusted had turned the corner and vanished out of sight, leaving him here with the gang of Punks.

John shrugged and walked towards the abandoned building, ready for confrontation. He'd probably get a few bruises from this, maybe a broken rib, but they'd heal. Knowing that, he could deal with the pain. Suddenly Trash and another large man materialized. They leaned against the building as the Spikers advanced.

"Great," John muttered to himself. "This should be interesting."

"Welcome," Trash said, grinning. "We've been expecting you."

TWENTY-TWO

JOHN STARED AT THE BROAD-SHOULDERED
Man with the tattoos. His complexion was dark-brown, his facial features rough. He was six-foot-three, and two-hundred pounds of solid muscle. His blue jeans had dotted stains of blood on them.

"You're Danny Boy!" John snapped.

"In the flesh," Danny said. He put his foot against the wall and adjusted his white hand wraps.

John noted his left arm was inked with dark-green boxing gloves. Tatted on his right shoulder was a tombstone with the words 'R.I.P. LITTLE MONSTER' etched across. The boxer stared at him with cold eyes.

Where is everybody? It's the middle of the day and there's no one around but these fuck holes. This must be a real bad area. Criminals running the street. No one else here to call the cops. This would be a horrible place to die in.

"Long time no see, Soul Brotha!" Trash grinned and taunted him. He was twirling a wooden bat in his hand. "You know, I haven't forgotten about the Pool Hall. I'm very upset with you right now."

"Let me ask you this, Sid Vicious; what the fuck makes you think I care?" John narrowed his eyes.

"We're gonna take you some place now. But before we do, we're gonna have some fun with you!"

Trash snapped his fingers. The four Punks with lead pipes surrounded him. Without warning one of them hit him hard in the head, the blow devastating. John collapsed to his knees. As if on cue the other three started beating him, hitting his legs, ribs, and knees.

Danny leaned over to Trash. "Yo son, you sure this is a good idea? Priest wants him alive."

"And he'll get him alive," he said, rolling his eyes, "I just wanna teach this asshole a lesson first."

"Yeah, but they keep goin' at this rate they gonna kill this boy."

He stare at him angrily. "You just do what you're told, Danny. Let me worry about that if that's what it comes to."

John spit up a glob of blood as they beat him severely. A heavy boot kicked his head, making his back and knees go numb. One of the Punks cackled insanely as he thwacked his spine with a pipe.

Alright John, I think you've taken enough. It's time to kick some Anarchy ass!

John opened his eyes and sprang to his feet, ignoring the blows. He grabbed one thug's pipe and clobbered him in the head with it. The Punk fell to the floor. He hit him again, breaking his knees. The Punk grabbed his knees and screamed in agony. He raised the pipe to hit again, but stopped when the others attacked him from behind.

"Shit," Trash muttered. He ran towards John to fight him.

Trash knew the remaining three could've beaten him to death, but he didn't want to take any chances. The young man had already proven himself in brawling. He still couldn't believe he'd single-handedly brought down all the fiends at Panaca Heights last night. He'd sold to them too many times to know how numerous and violent they were.

John dropped the pipe and grabbed one of the swinging Punks. He picked him up and threw him through one of the windows of the abandoned building. Screaming followed by a low thud erupted from the shitty building, then it stopped.

Trash hit him in the back, the cracking sound of the blow loud and frightening. Any normal human being would've been paralyzed or killed by a blow like that. The other two thugs went to work on his knees while Trash hit his arms and chest, hollering like a nut bag the whole time.

John dodged one of his swings and jumped high into the air, knocking him down with a spin kick. He grabbed the bat and swung viciously at another Punk, knocking every tooth out of his mouth in a single shot. He turned and hit the other one in the head. He swung again, hitting him in the chest, then the arms, then the knees.

He swung until he knocked the last one out. His wild breathing returned to normal and he could feel his body healing on the inside. Blood was no longer leaking from his mouth…he could feel his spine again.

"Hey son!"

John spun around and faced Danny. He was leaning against the wall of the abandoned building, unimpressed by the whole thing. He unfolded his arms, then leaned down and brushed the dirt off his white shell tops. He cleaned the black stripes, then grabbed a pipe from the ground and stood.

"You know, I never really liked usin' nothing like these." He held the pipe in his hands and stared at it. "Kinda takes the fun out it all. Nah mean?"

Danny Boy threw the pipe behind him. He stared at John for a second and grinned. He bounced around and started shadow-boxing, throwing quick combinations.

John nodded. He dropped the bat and moved towards the boxer. Adrenaline budded within him, leaking throughout his whole body. Gusts of wind blew past him and through the boarded-up building, the gusts making haunted-like whistling sounds.

They squared off with each other. John threw a jab at him. Danny smacked it down and hit him with two, then hooked off and threw a right. In a flash he was on his ass, staring up at the tatted henchman.

He jumped to his feet and put his guard up, then moved

in. He moved forward and doubled up on the jab, trying to set him up—and Danny disappeared. Confused, he glanced around.

Pop! Pop!

John felt his knees buckle when two hard punches smashed into his chin. Again, he was on his ass, looking up into a spinning sky. Wind continued to blow by, making the whole experience even more disorienting.

"You gotta do better than that, son!" Danny taunted. He bounced around and shadow-boxed some more. "That's all you got?"

He glowered at the hood. He scrambled to his feet and put his hands up. Trash glanced up at them, still lying on the street. As the two men fought he crawled away.

John threw three jabs and a right that were all blocked by Danny. He stepped to the side and threw a wide right, missing it horribly as the boxer ducked. Frustrated, he saw that the man had disappeared again.

Pop-pop-pop, BOW!

Danny hit him with a devastating combination, staggering him back. Fists and images of him flashed before John's eyes as the man backed him up, pummeling him. His left eye was swollen, and he could feel a mouse forming under his right one.

He somehow ducked his last two swings and ran backwards, trying to get his bearings back. *I'm losing* he thought. The boxer crept forward, dropping his hands to insult him. He vanished again, then popped up in front of his face.

Five solid rights hammered into John's body, knocking the wind out of him, but he refused to go down. They moved in a circle, looking for openings on each other. Two more rights slammed into his face. Then another. And another. Bloody and out of breath, he wondered how the wily henchman could land so many rights on him…then it dawned on him.

He's a southpaw! No wonder why I'm getting killed!

John stopped moving to his right and hopped back a few steps. Hands up he stood still, waiting for him to move in. Danny charged in with a right hand. He dodged left and hit the brawny man with a huge body shot.

Danny dropped his hands, surprised by the blow. John didn't hesitate. He got in close, chopping away at his body again, then came up with a hook; he ducked it, though. Danny came up with a rising uppercut, knocking him off his feet.

When John hopped up the boxer was already there, punching his face and body, hitting him with fifteen-piece combos. He landed a right on the boxer's chin, staggering him back. The boxer recovered and charged him. Once again he dodged to the left and went to his body, then faked a hook. When the boxer ducked he threw a low right, punching him in the nose.

He cheered inwardly when he caught a glimpse of the boxer's swollen eye. At last, he'd found a strategy that worked. Danny rushed in with lightning combos. John mustered up all of his rage and hit him back, trading blows with him.

They fought in the street, throwing face-splitting punches, beating each other to bloody pulps. Out of breath they slugged each other over and over again, neither one with their guards up. Danny caught him with three jabs, then landed a right to his body. He wound way back and threw a mighty hook.

John ducked the knockout swing. He smashed Danny with ten body shots, then hit him with an uppercut. Danny punched him repeatedly in the face but John ignored the blows, eating them as he charged forward. They traded blows again as they stepped out of the street. They fought on the sidewalk in front of the building.

Danny Boy slammed his fist into his jaw and threw a hook. John dodged it and caught him with a right, then landed an overwhelming hook on his jaw. The blow knocked the boxer off his feet.

John watched with triumph as the fighting menace crashed to the sidewalk and stayed there. Fists still balled he stood for a moment, staring at the unconscious man that was beating the tar out of him earlier.

Gotcha.

Loud police sirens pierced the air. John panicked when he realized that they weren't too far away. He pulled himself together and lurched forward. He jumped through the broken window and landed inside the building.

Black rats the size of his shoes scurried by him, hissing as they went. He got to his feet and ran across the rickety wooden floors, and spotted a set of stairs. In a flash he hit the stairs and sprinted upwards, taking them two at a time. He could hear the fuzz outside.

He ran down the piss-smelling halls and almost fell to the ground when he grabbed the collapsing railing. He busted into a door covered with yellow tape and shut it behind him. The room he was in was covered with trash and other filth.

A twenty-foot-tall window with broken glass was in front of him. He inched forward and glanced up at the jagged glass.

What happened here?

Angry voices from outside made him nervous. He fell to the dirty floor and crawled forward. He carefully peered over the window sill to see what was happening in the streets.

"Fuck you mufuckas!" Danny yelled.

Danny Boy was getting arrested outside. He was in handcuffs and resisting the cops as they shoved him into one of the squad cars. He counted three cars in all, surprised that they even came down to this crap-hole in the first place. The boxer continued to curse them as they slammed the door and radioed in to headquarters.

John kept watching them from the window. After a few

minutes the police jumped in their cars and sped away. He was lost to his thoughts, oblivious to the jagged, hefty-sized, piece of glass hanging from above.

What happened to that shit-head Trash? And who called the cops to begin with? It just doesn't make any sense.

Shhhik!

The large piece of glass from above broke and fell down towards him. John turned sideways and caught a glimpse of it in his tunnel vision. He tried to get out of the way, but he wasn't quick enough. The sharp glass fell on him, slicing into his throat, almost decapitating him.

He pulled the glass out of his neck and threw it to the wooden floor. He stumbled back, confused with how the world appeared sideways. A sickening thought settled in his stomach when he realized that his head and neck was hanging onto his body by a thin piece of skin and muscle.

Blood. Blood leaked from everywhere. Nothing made sense. The world took on a reddish-haze. Then a cloudy white. He grabbed at his neck and realized he was holding his Adam's Apple in his hand. He put it back in his neck and wiped warm, oozing liquid onto his pants.

Dying...I'm dy-ing...

Rivers of blood flowed into his mouth, making him choke. His heart beat irregularly, the rhythm unrecognizable. Red liquid leaked into his nose and eyes. The taste of his own blood made him nauseous. He fell to his knees and grabbed his head, trying to put it back on his body. The slightest tear would sever it forever.

Warm, sticky liquid was all over him, around him. Muscle tissue and skin fused together as the wound to his neck began to close. He fell on his back, shivering in a pool of his own blood. Panic tore through him when images of bloody soldiers stood in the room with him.

They were images of his Army friends and the enemy Falcon Army; except they weren't images at all...they were real. Men that had been blown in half, shot full of bullets, and missing limbs were around him now, closing in on him.

The dead soldiers reached out to him with scarlet hands, their eyes glazed over from death. He shook violently as they got closer. Closer. The pain was unbearable, like a hot sword burning into his head, burning even the blood on the floor from his wound.

Sounds of howling wolves filled the room. The howling turned into shrieks, and then loud ringing. Ringing in his ears. He covered them as he saw the color of the world turn gray. Then silver. Silver blood fell to the walls and crawled to the ceiling, raining down on him like drops of fire. And then the ringing stopped.

The dead soldiers slowly disappeared, then vanished altogether. The walls and floors weren't bleeding, and the ceiling no longer rained blood. His vision returned to normal, the color of the world restored. He rubbed his neck, relieved to find the wound had closed up.

His head was still attached to his body. He was alive. Slowly he pushed himself off the floor and stood on shaky legs. He suddenly felt very weak, like the life had literally been drained out of him. The feeling reminded him of the first time he'd been poisoned with radiation.

I almost...died. That's it, I almost died just now. One more tear and my head would've completely fallen off.

"So that's my weakness," he said, whispering to himself. "Decapitation."

John walked out of the abandoned building. He turned the corner and held onto the wall, still feeling drained. Twenty feet ahead of him was a 1970 Coupe Deville, parked next to the curb. He crept towards the two-door sedan, surprised to find a Punk inside of it. The thug was passed out behind the wheel.

John carefully opened the door and pulled him out, and gently laid him on the street. He hopped in the Coupe and pulled off, suddenly feeling more afraid than he'd ever felt in his life.

TWENTY-THREE

"I WANT HIM FUCKING DEAD!"
Priest yelled. He paced the room in the abandoned apartment building. There was a broken TV set in the corner. He charged towards it. Frightened gangsters scattered as he swung his bat, demolishing it to pieces.

"Hey man, take it easy!" Trash yelled, trying to calm him down. Psycho stood beside him and watched as their leader went berserk.

He glanced around the room, searching for something else to break, and caught a glimpse of his idiot followers. They stared at him with stupid looks on their faces. Suddenly he felt the urge to smash their fucking faces in, to beat them until they stopped moving.

"Motherfuckers!"

He ran to the cracked window and hit it, smashing the glass, causing it to explode and shatter to the ground below. In a fit of uncontrolled fury he turned and blindly swung, striking one of his own Punks in the head, killing him instantly. Blood gushed from the thug's head and decorated the walls behind him as he fell to the ground.

"Priest!" Trash ran over and grabbed his arm.

Psycho grabbed his other one. They tried calming him down as other terrified Spikers ran out of the room. He glared at them madly, his eyes crazy and animal-like. Trash spoke up again.

"Danny Boy is gone! Alright? He's gone man, the cops

got him. Now I *told* you we shoulda' taken care of this kid, but you wouldn't listen! And now this is the result."

Priest's eyes were homicidal. He glared at Trash, and for a split second gave serious thought to killing him right then and there. He blinked for a few seconds. When his head cleared he pushed past them.

"Follow me."

The Punks followed him out of the room. The three of them ran downstairs and left the abandoned apartment complex. They moved right, then turned left and walked past Enna's, a massage parlor that stood in between the complex and the Skyline Apartment building.

When they saw Priest moving towards Skyline, every Punk selling crack stopped what they were doing and followed him in. He turned and stood in the lobby, waiting for the rest of Anarchy to make their way in. The one's that couldn't fit into the lobby stood by the windows outside, peering in. Others stood in the streets, straining to hear their leader. Hundreds of eyes were on him, waiting on him like he was the second coming.

"One man!" Priest yelled, his voice echoing off the walls. He glared at everyone.

"Comes into BayView...my city, your city, and tries to fuck around. He blows up the Pool Hall. He gets our connection at LEGZ pinched. He takes Danny Boy away from us? One man does this to you!"

He raised his bat high and brought it down, smashing it into the stained floor. Bits of white tile cracked and flew outwards.

"I want John Cutter dead! I want this motherfucker dead! Dead! *DEAD*! When you see him you don't ask questions, you don't give him a beating, you don't catch him—you kill him! You rip that motherfuckers skull apart!"

Punks cheered at his words. Bats, pipes, and chains were raised in the air as a salute.

"Who are we?" Priest asked, his voice raspy. He raised his bat over his head.

"*Anarchy!*" the Punks chanted.

"Who are we?"

"*Anarchy!*"

"Who the fuck are *we*?"

"*Anarchy! Anarchy! Anarchy!*"

Anarchy jumped around and chanted. They were lost in a frenzy. They smashed into each other, pushing, shoving, hollering.

"Bring me his head!" Priest yelled.

Anarchy charged out into the streets, ready to shed blood.

John bent the corner and sped down Montbello Street. Warm air blew past him as he drove with the windows down, cursing the broken AC. He pulled his bloody shirt off and threw it out the window. Too many thoughts flooded his mind, so he hurried to Summerville.

You have to be careful, John. You're not invincible like you once thought. I guess it makes sense, though. Get your head cut off and you're done. But what if I get shot in the head? Can I die that way, too? Or does it have to be decapitation? I wonder.

He stopped in front of Summerville Heights and hopped out the car. He raced up the stairs and banged on her door.

"April? Open up, it's me!"

There was a moment of hesitation. The door opened. She let him in and slammed it behind her.

"Where's your key?" she asked, her eyes wide.

"I left it here." He ran to the bathroom and grabbed a fresh t-shirt from under the sink. He put it on and ran back out to the living room, scooped up his black bag, and put it on his shoulders. He looked at her and smiled inwardly, glad to see the 9-mm in her hand.

"Let's go."

She quickly grabbed her purse. "Okay. Let me get some change for the subway—"

"Forget it," he said. He grabbed her wrist and pulled her to the door. "You don't need that."

She frowned as he opened the door. "How are we supposed to get to KingStreet then, walk? Are you crazy?"

"Don't worry about that, just come on."

He glanced around the apartment one last time, and wondered if he'd ever see it again. He signed and stepped out, waiting for her to lock the door.

They ran down the stairs and brushed past a few meddling winos. She froze when they got to the sidewalk.

"John…where did you get this?"

He opened the door to the passenger's side and hurled the heavy bag to the back seat. He looked back at her, smiling. "Hop in."

She stared at the rally-green metallic car. She hesitated a moment, not sure what to do. He ran around to the driver's side and saw the baffled look on her face; he had the sinking feeling that she wasn't going to get in. Irritated, he thought about yelling at her, then stopped when she rushed to his side.

"Okay. But I'm driving."

Thank fucking goodness. I'm tired of arguing.

John ran over to the passenger's side and jumped in, then slammed the door shut. A grin slowly spread across his face. His feet needed a rest, and it was a good feeling not to have to take the subway.

April started the ignition and peeled off, tires screeching. She weaved in and out of traffic, ignoring the horns and cursing of the other drivers.

"Can't believe I'm doing this," she said, muttering under her breath. She turned another corner and sped up to beat the light.

"What?" John asked. He checked the side mirror for cops.

"I haven't been to work all day because some lunatic tried to kill me last night. The gang that's after you is probably after me now, and now I'm driving some stolen car to their hide-out."

He nodded thoughtfully. "Yeah. Sounds like your year is off to a good start."

"Not funny, John! Do you realize that my career could be in jeopardy for this? I know that you're supposed to be some big, bad vigilante with retirement checks from the government, but I have to work for a living!"

He sighed. "Listen I'm sorry I dragged you into this. But there was no other way, okay? If we don't put a stop to Priest's gang then nobody will. Besides, you know as well as I do that it's only a matter of time before this shit shows up at your door. I mean look at what happened to you in the tunnels last night."

John saw her frown, obviously not agreeing with him. He was surprised when she didn't say anything to his last statement. He was right and she knew it, that's why she didn't respond.

"Why are your jeans all bloody?" she asked. She stopped at the red light.

John closed his eyes and ran his fingers through his wavy, black hair. "You really don't want to know."

"And who did you steal this car from? Al Capone?"

"What?"

She nodded to the backseat. "Look at all that shit!"

John followed her gaze to the floor of the backseat. He gasped when he saw two M-16s, a brown shotgun, and dozens of magazines. He glanced back at her, unsure of how to answer—

—and felt his heart freeze in his chest when he saw a brown S Coupe pull up beside her. The Coupe was filled with

Anarchy. A goon on the passenger's side had a Snub-Nose aimed at her head.

"Get down!" John heard himself yell.

John grabbed her head and forced her down as bullets tore into the car. He reached behind him and grabbed the black bag. He pulled out the .380 and the 44 Magnum. The Punk stopped firing. He glanced over to see him reloading.

"Drive!"

April floored it. Tires screeching they sped off. The brown Coupe caught up with them, and the windows on its right side were rolled down with Punks hanging half-way out of them. They fired at April.

John leaned half-way out of his window and faced them as she swerved in the traffic. He blasted back at them. He shot the one leaning out the window with the Snub Nose. The goon dropped his gun and fell out. A sickening crunch filled the air as other cars rolled over his body.

John shot the driver in the head. The car spun wildly and flipped up in the air, then crashed to the ground. Other cars piled into it, ending the rest of the Punks inside.

"Look out!" April screamed.

A blue Chevy Caprice pulled up to their right. Two goons with mohawks leaned out the windows. Armed with Mac-10s they opened fire, peppering the side of the Coupe Deville.

"Hold it steady!" John yelled over the gunfire. He opened up on them, his Snub Nose and 44 jumping in his hands.

A bullet from his Magnum slammed into the Punk in the backseat. He dropped his Mac and slumped out the window, hanging out of the speeding car. He aimed at the Chevy's tires. He squeezed the trigger and blew them out.

The blue Chevy swerved violently, then flipped over twenty-eight times. April sped away and swerved around the cars, screaming at the other drivers to move.

"We got company!" John aimed his guns at two Fleetwood Broughams behind them.

The red Broughams sped up and drove on either side of them. John glanced in both of the cars; the one on April's side had three goons in it, the one on his filled with four. The goon's in the car to his right blasted their automatic pistols.

He shot two goons with his 44, blowing both of them out of the car, then shot the one in the passenger seat with his .380. He shot the driver twice with his 44, then shot the hood of the red Brougham. The car screeched and did a three-sixty; it exploded in the traffic. By some miracle it didn't take any other cars out.

"Ah!"

"John!" April shouted. One of the bullets hit him.

The damn Punks to the left of them started shooting at them. He ducked back into the Coupe and dropped his guns to the floor. He turned and reached behind the seat.

"I'm alright," he said, grabbing an M-16, "they just grazed me. Keep driving!"

He poked out the window and leaned over the hood, facing left. He opened up on the shooting Punks, trading bullets with them. Bullets from his M-16 decorated the side of their Fleetwood, but he couldn't tell if he'd hit any of them. A 9-mm slug zipped by his head, making him flinch.

The red Brougham sped off, leaving them in the dust. He ducked back into the car.

"Follow them, April! Don't loose them!"

She nodded, pushing the pedal to the floor. The green Coupe lurched forward, weaving in and out of traffic, missing other drivers by inches. They barreled down KingStreet, following the fleeing goons.

April shrieked as she sped past the Fun Times Arcade. KingStreet was littered with Anarchy. Punks came out of alleys and burned-down buildings, armed with bricks and bats.

"Oh, shit!" she screamed. She hit one of the Punks

with the car. She panicked as she hit another one, running over him.

John shook his head. "Don't worry about it! Fuck em', run em' over!"

April ran over twelve more. As John leaned out his window with his M-16 she purposely hit more of them, running over their bodies. Sounds of breaking bones filled the air as the goon's crunched under the tires. He opened up on the others with a hail of gunfire, mowing them down with his rifle.

Glass windows shattered as he squeezed the trigger. Bullets slammed into the body of the Coupe and flew by him. Gang members ran out of High Times Liquor Store and from around the Good Times Cineplex, blasting guns. He aimed up and shot five of them off the roof of the burned-out Cineplex.

Punks emerged from everywhere, shooting at them with pistols and automatic rifles. April took her 9-mm out of her waistband. She pointed it out the window, shooting at them as she drove by.

April and John blasted at the scum, blowing them away as she sped down the war zone of KingStreet. John emptied the rest of his magazine into one's face, then ducked in the car again. He snatched a grenade out of his bag.

"Eat this, muthafuckas!"

He pulled the pin and tossed it out the window at a cluster of thugs. It exploded on impact, blowing them into a liquid cloud of blood. The red Brougham in front of them tried speeding away.

"Catch up with them!" he commanded. He grabbed three grenades and pulled the pins out.

April sped up, smashing into a Punk in the street, sending him flying through the air. She pulled up to the right side of the Brougham. The three Punks scowled over at them. They raised their pistols. John smiled at them and tossed the grenades into their car.

April slammed on the brakes and let the Fleetwood Brougham speed forward. Six seconds later it exploded. The red car slammed into the abandoned building to the right side of Enna's Massage Parlor.

John tossed two more grenades out the window, then slapped a fresh magazine into the M-16. He leaned out the window, spraying. Armed Punks twitched and shook as bullets hit them, sending them to a dancing death.

Crash! Crash!

The back window exploded inwards as the Punks shot at them. A lone slug slammed into the windshield, causing a large crack to spider web, making it hard for April to see. John grabbed three grenades and some cartridges from his bag. He unlocked the door.

"Jump out the car!"

She looked at him in disbelief. "Are you fucking nuts?"

"It's not safe to drive anymore! Jump out!"

She bit her lip and stared at him, her eyes wide. She unlocked her door. Bullets riddled the car as she steered it to the left. They glanced away from each other and opened their doors, jumping out at the same time.

John hit the street hard and rolled to the right. He sat up and watched the Coupe Deville speed down the street. A lone bullet hit the gas tank, and an earth-shattering boom rocked the ground as it exploded into a yellow flame. Seconds later he scrambled to his feet and glanced around.

"April?"

"I'm okay!"

He searched for the voice that answered him, and caught movement out the corner of his eye. He glanced to his left, spotting her in the street. He ran over to her, ducking shots.

John reached out and helped her up. She had a few cuts and bruises on her arms, but other than that, she'd be okay.

KA-BOOM!

The Brougham that hit the abandoned building earlier exploded again. Fire climbed the building's walls, burning the windows and floors. Flaming goons ran out of the building, shooting their pistols aimlessly.

Tat-tat-tat!

John shot them down with his rifle, moving his gun in a sweeping motion. April turned around and blasted her 9.

The Spikers had them surrounded. John killed seven more then re-loaded the M-16.

"I'm out!" April shouted, glancing over her shoulder.

He handed her a clip and the M-16. "Here, take this."

Ahead of them to the left stood the Skyline Apartments. Dozens of Spikers armed with handguns piled out. April covered John while he re-loaded his Magnum and .380. They ran forward, shooting down goons, blowing their chests apart. Hundreds more ran out, firing at them.

John took a grenade from his pocket and pulled the pin. He threw it at the Punk mob. They scattered like roaches when it hit the ground.

Ka-Boom!

Chunks of concrete and tar flew up, then rained to the ground. John glanced up at Skyline. Spikers were shooting at them from every window. They charged forward dauntlessly, putting holes in anything that moved toward them. Trash and Psycho appeared in the Skyline entrance, armed with Uzis.

"You and your girlfriend are fucked!" Psycho hollered. "I'm gonna kill you!"

April froze in her tracks, ignoring the gunshots going off around her. "That voice." She nudged John's shoulder. "That's him! That's the one who killed Charlie!"

John's jaw dropped. He frowned, oblivious to the bullets that almost hit him. The knot in his chest returned, only this time it felt bigger. He glanced away from her and glared at Psycho. He raised his guns up and ran forward, blasting away at them. April turned and shot the Punks behind her away, covering his back.

"Come on, dude!" Trash hollered. He cackled like a maniac. "Come on!"

Trash and Psycho shrank back inside, disappearing into the building.

John ran into the lobby. The reeking odor inside made the back of his throat lock. He ignored his nausea and ran towards the steps.

Tat-tat-tat-tat-tat-tat-tat-tat!

Trash appeared at the top of the steps, shooting at them. April dove to the right for cover while John moved forward, unfazed by his assault. He raised his guns.

"Come on Soul Brotha, show me what you got! Come on, John! Come here, John! Cuh-mon, cuh-mere, cu-mon motherfucker!"

Blam, BLAM! Blam, BLAM!

John's guns exploded. Trash flew backwards and slammed into the wall. Blood spurted from his chest and splashed the wall behind him.

"Auuugh!"

Trash stumbled forward and stood at the top of the steps. April was on her feet now. She brushed past John and pointed the M-16 at the bloody Punk. She squeezed the trigger, watching the bullets fly into his body.

Trash dropped his Uzi and shook violently as the rounds tore away his flesh. Blood spewed from his mouth, staining his white t-shirt, dotting his black boots. She kept shooting him as he fell down the stairs. He crashed to the bottom, breaking his neck.

April stepped forward, still shooting his body. She stopped in front of the Punk and moved her gun in a sweeping motion, filling him full of holes. John stepped up and stood next to her. He emptied his .380 into him as she sprayed him with the M-16.

They stopped firing and stared down at him. Blood pooled from Trash like a wild river. Every inch of his body was covered with leaking holes.

Crackling gunfire jolted them out of their daze, giving them no time to revel in his death. Psycho shot at them from above, then ran up to the third floor. They ducked and ran up the stairs. Bullets whizzed past them and splintered the floors and railings.

John and April made it to the second floor. He pointed to the rotting set of stairs forty feet ahead of them. They crept forward, moving down the blazing hallway. Sweat oozed out of his pores and ran down his body. A door to the left of them swung open.

"Get down!" John yelled. He pushed her away and dove backwards, catching a feint glimpse of the room full of thugs.

The Spikers let loose with a sea of bullets. One of them reached out and closed the door. John jumped up and signaled April to stay down. To the right of him was a red fire extinguisher attached to the wall. He grabbed it and pressed his back against the wall, then opened the door.

Fwoosh!

A white cloud filled the room full of Spikers. He threw the extinguisher inside and grabbed a grenade from his pocket. He pulled the pin and threw it in, then slammed the door shut. Shouting and gunfire erupted from the room as he scooped his guns up and ran over to April.

"Come on!"

They took off down the hallway, desperately trying to reach the stairs. They ran up, taking the steps three at a time.

KA-BLOOM!

Pieces of the door splintered outwards. The hallway to the second floor filled up with billowing smoke. They ran down the hall of the third floor. Bullets flew threw the doors as Punks within the rooms fired. John and April shot blindly at the doors in the hall, moving at top speed. The brown door to Room 328 flew open, and out stepped a Spiker.

He knocked the guns out of John's hands and grabbed him by the collar. The pale, cracked-out goon slammed him into the railing, trying to push him over. He grabbed a grenade and pulled the pin, then shoved it in the Spiker's leather pants.

John grabbed him and spun him around. He snatched his 44 from the ground, then shot the goon in the stomach. The goon grabbed his gut and fell over the railing. He hollered all the way down until he exploded.

"Come on up here, John!" Psycho yelled, shooting at them from above. "I'll send you home in a body bag!"

John and April dove in different directions as he shot at them. She laid on the floor and covered her head while John re-loaded his .380.

"Hey John, guess what? You know your friend Charlie? I killed him John! I blew his brains all over the place!"

He re-loaded his 44. The knot in his chest spread within him until he felt it all over. He stood and shot upwards, emptying his .380. Uzi bullets answered him back, missing him narrowly.

"You wanna know something else about your friend? He died beautifully, John! I saw the inside of his skull before he crossed over to the other world! He cried out like a baby when the bullets hit his body, John! I got him, I got him, he *died!*"

John's hands shook. The insults fueled his rage. He stood and moved up the stairs, pressing his back against the wall. He inched forward and came to the fourth floor. He turned and glanced down the hallway, spotting Psycho leaning over the wooden railing. To the Punk's left stood a dirty, six-foot window.

Psycho stopped yelling and turned. He glared at John as he walked slowly towards him. He raised his Uzi and backed up a few steps. He shouted, his threats frog-ish and incomprehensible.

"I'm not afraid of you, motherfucker! So come on!"

John didn't reply. His entire body trembled and he kept moving forward. Psycho's left eye twitched as he raised his gun slightly, aiming it at his head.

"I'm gonna send you to meet your friend now, John! You can join him in hell!"

John raised his 44 and fired. The bullet smacked into Psycho's left shoulder. His glassy eyes widened as his shoulder exploded into a crimson cloud. He took another step and blasted again, hitting his chest. He fired another shot. Then another...and another.

Each blast forced Psycho back to the window. Red liquid bubbled from his mouth and sprayed outwards as the Magnum rounds tore into his heroin-ravaged body. John raised his 44 higher and shot him in the head, blowing his forehead completely away, spilling his brains down his face.

Psycho flew through the window behind him and spiraled to the ground, shooting his Uzi as he fell. The Uzi fire abruptly stopped. A wet *thud* was the next sound he heard.

John slowly walked to the shattered window and glanced down, spotting Psycho's twisted, broken body on the street.

"That's for Charlie," he said, his voice trembling.

Within seconds the tenseness in his body dissolved. Suddenly the tightness in his chest melted away, leaving him all together. He stared at the murderer again, and thought of his friend.

"That's for you, Charlie. For you."

He saw movement out the corner of his eye. April stood next to him. She followed his gaze to the dead body below.

"You got him, huh?"

"Yeah," he said, not looking at her.

They stood in silence for a moment, marveling at the gory view. She reached out and squeezed his shoulder. He nodded and they backed away from the window. They turned around and slowly walked past the doors in the hallway, ready to leave Skyline.

Crash!

Michael Priest busted through the door behind them, obliterating it into infinite pieces. He put his bat around April's neck. She dropped her M-16 over the railing and grabbed at his hands.

"Guess what fuckhead, I'm still here!" He cackled insanely as he dragged her towards the stairs going to the fifth floor.

John frowned. He reached in his pocket and pulled out his last Magnum cartridge. "Let her go Priest!"

He looked at him in disbelief. "No way, asshole! You must be out of your fucking mind to think you can come down here and fuck with me!"

He quickly loaded his gun and moved towards them. "Let her go! This is between you and me, and you know it. She ain't got nothing to do with this. Take me instead!"

John panicked when he saw the way he was dragging April up the stairs. He was choking her with the bat. Her face was turning a deep blue. Her eyes looked like they were going to pop out of her head. Her shoes scuffed the stairs as they staggered upwards.

"John," April weakly called out to him. Her eyes narrowed, and were a blink away from closing.

Rage boiled within John when he saw her blue face getting darker. She was going to die if he didn't act. He pointed the gun at him, but hesitated. He couldn't get a clear shot.

"Goddamn you Priest, let her go! I'll blow your brains out!"

"Why don't you take the shot? Go ahead, tuff guy!"

He grinned wickedly, knowing that John wouldn't risk hitting her. They topped the fifth floor and backed up towards the next set of stairs.

"Let her go and deal with me!" John shouted. The 44 trembled in his sweaty hands.

"Why don't you take the shot?"

"Fuck you!"

"Take the shot!"

April mustered up the little strength she had left and elbowed him hard in the stomach. Priest's blue eyes widened with shock. He dropped the bat and let her go. A sinister frown formed on his face.

"Fucking bitch!" He cocked his hand back and slapped her, knocking her over the railing. He snatched his bat from the floor and sprinted up the stairs.

"No!" John sprinted to the railing and reached out, but it was too late. He leaned over and searched, but he couldn't see her.

He turned and took off up the stairs, taking no time to mourn. Shots rang out from the sixth floor above him, the slugs hitting his body. He ignored them, sprinting upwards, blowing the Spikers away. He shot three of them to hell, then blasted another one in the face as he made it to the sixth floor.

Priest was at the other end of the hall. He smiled, then disappeared up the stairs. A random Punk struck him in the back with a lead pipe. John turned and put the 44 to his face, blowing his head off his body. He dropped the gun and spun around.

"Get back, motherfucker!" A green-haired freak popped up in front of him, aiming a pistol to his face.

John knocked the gun out of his hand and grabbed behind the man's legs. He flipped him over the railing, sending him to a plummeting death.

"*Priest!*" he cried out, the words rasping in his throat.

He sprinted up the stairs and reached for the last door.

TWENTY-FOUR

JOHN BURST THROUGH THE DOOR TO THE roof. Consumed with malice he glanced around the rooftop, searching for Priest. Murder was the only thing on his mind. He wanted to kill him. He wanted to beat the blood out of his body. He thought about how he'd knocked April over the railing.

Sadness mixed with his rage. He tried to ignore his feelings, but couldn't. His will to kill took over. It was the only thing he had left inside, the only thing driving him to go on.

He decided that after he killed Priest he'd kill the rest of his underlings, too. None of them would survive. They would all pay, even if it meant hunting every single one of them down for the rest of his life.

"Priest!" He leaned back and cocked his head towards the sky. "Come out and face me, Priest! You and me, let's finish it now!"

Wham!

Sharp pain exploded inside of his skull as an aluminum bat smashed the back of his skull. Once again, he'd been careless. He failed to use street smarts, and now he was going to pay. He grabbed his head and collapsed to the ground.

More pain erupted as Priest hit him in the back. He struck his arms with the unbreakable weapon. He struck his leg next, smashing the bone. John crawled forward and bent his knees, trying to get up.

"You never give up, do you John? You never...fucking give up!"

Priest kicked him hard in his ribs, forcing him back down. He kicked him again and again, yelling as he did so.

"You're a stupid motherfucker! What made you think you could go against me, huh? What? I know you didn't think you could stop me. I know you didn't think you could take over!"

He kicked John in the mouth, the boot crushing his jaw. He hit him with the bat and stomped him repeatedly, lost in a frenzy of hate.

"Who sent you down here to stop me, huh? Was it Gutter Street? Was it Torrio? Tell me Cutter. Tell me before you die!"

While John was getting stomped he cursed himself for telling Priest his last name in the warehouse. *Why did you do that?* he wondered. It could've been a slip of the tongue. Or maybe it was because he'd gotten beaten so bad that night that his brain had stopped working properly, and he thought it was a good idea to tell him.

Whatever the reason, it didn't matter now. Just another example of him not using his head.

"Tell me who sent you," he hissed. He hit him with the bat, then kicked him again. "Hurry and tell me...so I can kill you like I did that bitch friend of yours!"

John clenched his teeth. Every kick sent an image of April into his mind.

"Tell me!"

John thought about the first night she'd invited him back to her apartment in Summerville.

"Tell me!"

He thought about the night they'd stayed up talking, and how she'd offered him tea.

"Tell me!"

He remembered her sunshine smile, and how he'd

never get to see it again.

"Grrraaaaa!" A savage growl rumbled out of John's throat. An unexplainable emotion took over his body, giving him strength, numbing him to the pain.

Priest raised the aluminum bat that had killed so many in the past high over his head. He swung it down fast—

—but John reached out and caught it. He slowly rose from the ground and stood to his full height, glaring up at him. The Punk shivered. He tried to snatch the bat away from him, but it was no use. His grip was too strong.

John snatched it away from *him*. The king of BayView City was now backing away, shaking with fear. He took a mighty swing, hitting him in his ugly face. He swung on him again.

"You—"

He swung again.

"—are"

He swung again, knocking blood out of his mouth.

"—finished!"

He wound back to hit the staggering street lord again. Seething, he got ready to swing, squeezing the bat in his hands. He hesitated for a few seconds, then spun around in a circle and hurled it over the roof. He dropped his hands and turned to face him.

"Make your move, Priest."

He shook his head, clearing it. He glared at John and lunged at him, swinging madly.

John dodged one of his haymakers and punched him. He followed up with an upper-cut, staggering him back, then slipped the jab. He hit him with two quick jabs, landed a right to his cheek, then went to his body. He came up and hooked him in the face, the force of the blow knocking him down.

Priest got to his feet, wobbling around. He rushed John and grabbed him, getting him in a reverse headlock. He kneed him three times, then hit him with an elbow smash. He locked his fingers, raised his hands up, then hit him with a hammer fist.

He raised his hands again, but John punched him in the chest. He swung hard, slugging Priest with everything he had, knocking him backwards to the edge of the roof.

Priest fell to his knees. He was only an inch away from being knocked over. John cocked his fist back.

"Go ahead then," he said. A smile broke out on his bloody face. "Do it."

He stared at him a moment, his fist still raised. All of a sudden he heard sirens in the distance. The police were on their way. If he was going to kill him, he had to do it now.

"Do it you idiot!" he hollered to the top of his lungs. "What are you waiting for? Kill me you motherfucker! You better kill me know…or I will come after you, you believe it! So finish it now while you got the chance, you fucking pussy. Do it!"

The cops were getting closer. They would be at Skyline any minute now. He lowered his fist and unclenched it.

"Nah, Priest. I got a better idea."

John opened the door and slowly descended to the fifth floor. If he didn't hurry up and leave, the police would haul his ass off to jail. Somehow he didn't care, going to the clink didn't phase him. None of that mattered…now that April was gone. He should have protected her.

No, you shouldn't have brought her with you in the first place. If you'd have left her out of this she'd still be alive, John.

He realized that gunshots to his head wouldn't kill him, but that didn't matter, either. He remembered how he'd almost died earlier in the abandoned building. He wished that he had been decapitated. His shoulders sagged as he inched towards the stairs.

"John?"

His heart jumped when he thought he heard a voice. "April? Is that you?"

Nah it can't be. She's dead man, you're crackin' up!

"John please help me."

He flinched at the sound of her voice, and realized that he wasn't hearing things. It was her!

"April where are you?"

"Down here. Please hurry!"

"Hold on, I'm on my way!"

He sprinted down the stairs, almost busting his ass in the process. He followed her voice until he got to the third floor. He got to the wooden railings and glanced down—and was thrilled to see her hanging onto the ledge. She glanced up at him, her face sweaty and frantic.

"Jesus Christ, how long have you been hanging from there?"

She glared at him. "Never mind that! Would you just help me?"

John leaned over the railing and reached down. He grabbed her sweaty hands and heaved her up, yanking her to safety. They fell backwards and collapsed to the floor. He sighed with relief, and wondered how she could hang on that long. If he'd been on the roof for just one more moment she would have fell to her death. He sat up quickly.

"Let's get out of here! Any minute now this place will be swarming with cops, and we don't want to be around for that."

They got up and ran down the stairs, hoping to make it to the tunnels in time.

TWENTY-FIVE

CAL HOUSTON AND MAD DOG WATCHED THE city's chaos from the Bryce Tower. KingStreet was crawling with cops, it was not the best place for a criminal to be right now. Dozens of Anarchy members were being hand-cuffed and shoved into squad cars.

"Look at this shit," Mad Dog said, "this is crazy!"

Cal stared through the binoculars, enjoying Anarchy's fall. "Relax, Dog. Everything's cool."

"How is it cool?" He scratched his long, black beard and paced the roof. "It looks pretty fucking far from cool to me!"

"Take it easy, Dog." He handed him the binoculars. "This is a good thing. Trust me."

He took them and kept protesting. "How is it a good thing, brother? Cops are everywhere in the city, there's probably going to be a drought season now. All the key players are finished."

"Not all the key players."

He looked at him, curious by what he meant. He pointed to the city, gesturing for him to look through the binoculars again.

"You see Mad Dog, this is the perfect opportunity for us. Why? Because for one reason the biggest gang in BayView is being cut in half right now. Most of Anarchy is being arrested as we speak, making it easier for new blood to move in and take over. Two, there's a major war going on right now; a war between Gutter Street Mafia and the Anarchy Punks. Their numbers will decrease when they slaughter each other. And three, so what if the cops are all over the city?

Pretty soon they're going to be arresting so many gang members, they'll be too busy to worry about us. Right now they don't even know we *exist*."

He handed the field glasses back to him. He let his words roll over in his head for a few moments, then nodded. "So when do we make a move?"

Cal Houston peered through the binoculars. He nodded and smiled.

"When they finish killing each other. Then we'll move in and pick up the pieces from the fallout."

EPILOGUE

JOHN LEANED BACK IN THE HARD SEAT, frowning at the discomfort. He wrinkled his nose up when he caught a whiff of the piss-infested floors. Crack pipes and old newspapers littered the ground and seats around them. Graffiti of different gangs decorated the windows and walls.

Well, it's official: we're riding the train again. Damn I hate the subway. Why did we have to lose that car?

April sat next to him, cracking her knuckles. His attitude brightened as he looked at her. He reminded himself that things could've turned out a lot worse. The fact that she'd survived was probably the second greatest thing that happened today. Her black hair was wild, and her tank-top and shorts were covered in grime.

She was a mess. They both were, he could only imagine what he looked like. Glancing around the train he was grateful that they were the only two aboard. He didn't feel like being around anyone else but her.

The guns, the gangs, the explosions…they'd basically been through a war. They had killed people and almost been killed themselves. She'd helped him out immensely.

April had been there for him since day one. She never judged him or looked down on him because of his problems…unlike his friends back home.

As far as he was concerned he had no more friends back home. She was his only friend. He glanced around.

It was a blessing that they were alone on the train. He'd felt the same way after being in a firefight with his Army buddies. After going through something like that it was hard to be around civilians again. It was hard to relate to them.

He grimaced inwardly when he caught a glimpse of the Anarchy sign. It was spray-painted everywhere, just like the other gang graffiti. He thought about Michael Priest, and how he'd decided to spare his life on the roof and let the cops find him. Killing him would have been too easy. Priest was addicted to running wild in the streets. Letting the cops lock him up and take away his freedom was the greatest punishment of all; greater than death.

April yawned next to him. She laid her head on his shoulder and closed her eyes. They hadn't said a word to each other since they'd snuck onto the train. Like him, she was too exhausted to talk. As they rode in silence, he thought about the first greatest thing that happened today; avenging Charlie.

We got em', Charlie...we got em'!

John closed his eyes and smiled as April drifted off. He was finally at peace.

ON SALE NOW!

CODE RED THE SEASON OF EVIL

NO ONE, IS SAFE...

CODE RED PRODUCTIONS
ORDER ONLINE www.createspace.com
OR CALL 1 (866) 356-2154

CHECK OUT CODE RED THE SEASON OF EVIL AT
YOUTUBE.COM

COMING SOON!

CODE RED 2
BY JOSHUA SARGENT

BE ON THE LOOKOUT FOR
OUTLAW 2

COMING FEBRUARY 1, 2013

OUTLAW

CITY OF FEAR

...stay inside

AUTHOR'S NOTE

The author of this novel does not condone violence in any way, shape, or fashion. OUTLAW CITY OF FEAR is intended for entertainment purposes only, and in no way should this material be imitated in real life.

Made in the USA
Charleston, SC
11 September 2013